DEDICATION

To Leslie Flood

FIRST PRINTING, MAY 1977

1 2 3 4 5 6 7 8 9

PRINTED IN U.S.A.

DELUSIA

Would death never end? Kalin smiled, her hair a rippling flame. She vanished as Earl took a step towards her and he stumbled and fell to a knee, hands outstretched.

The promenade, once empty, was now thronged with figures. Men, women, some strange, others vaguely familiar, a few seeming to gain solidity as he watched. The man he had fought on Harald, eyes glazing in hatred as he died. The gentle face of Armand Ramhed, the ruined one of his assassin, the sly eyes of an old woman from . . . from . . . and then, shockingly, he was looking at himself.

A man lying pale and limp and apparently dead. A man who dissolved and rose and stood tall and menacing in a scarlet robe.

Cyber Broge, his face like a skull, bone which smiled.

"There's no escape, Dumarest. We are too powerful. We shall find you and, when we do, you will pay." The even tones echoed as if rolling down a corridor. "Pay . . . pay . . . pay. . . ."

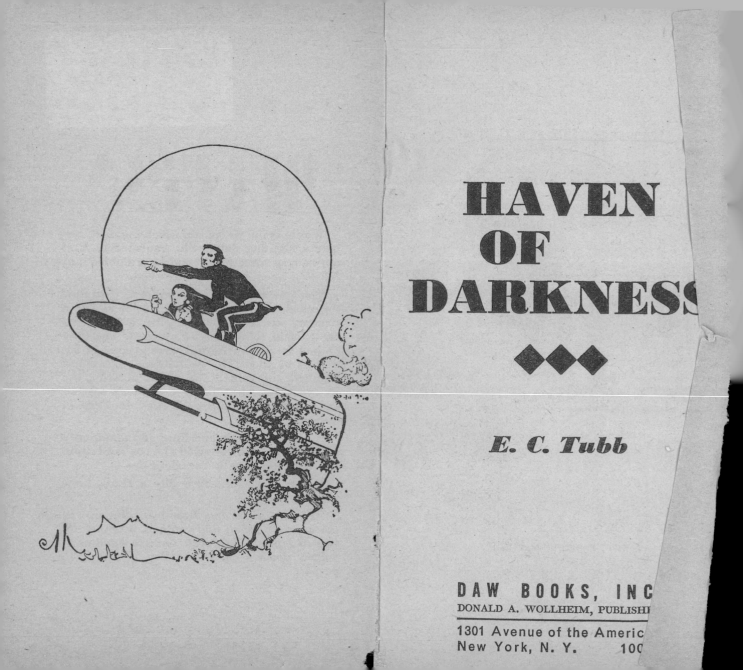

HAVEN
OF
DARKNESS

◆◆

E. C. Tubb

DAW BOOKS, INC.

DONALD A. WOLLHEIM, PUBLISHER

1301 Avenue of the Americas

New York, N. Y.   10019

HAVEN
OF
DARKNESS

Chapter ONE

~~~~~~~~~~~~~~~~~~~~~~~~~~~~~~~~~~~~

Delusia came unexpectedly so that she continued riding towards the north, forgetting the passage of time in the stimulating conversation with Charles. He looked well as he rode easily at her side, his clothes the same as she remembered him wearing when, shortly after they had first met, he had attended her on a hunt. The bag had been negligible; some vermin tossed aside on the homeward journey, but the pleasure had been great. They had wandered, hands touching, talking of a variety of things with a irresistible torrent of words. Normally shy she had found a release in his presence while he, perhaps amused at her young eager attention, had relaxed the guard he usually wore.

Now, riding close to her side, he was the same suave, charming man she had known when little more than a girl. A long time ago now and she had known him when he looked other than he did at the moment. There had been lines tracing the smooth curve of his cheek and a sagging of the flesh beneath the chin. The old, familiar manner had become crusted with accumulated layers of distrust and, when he had finally died, killed in some stupid quarrel, he had resembled an old and tired man rather than the youth she chose to remember.

"Charles!" She lifted her whip and pointed ahead to where a narrow cleft showed in the bleak wall of the Iron Mountains. "That gulley, you see it? The first to reach it claims a forfeit. Go!"

A childish game and one she hadn't played for years now and she had a moment's wonder as to why she should choose to play it now. A return to her youth, perhaps, her childhood? The fiction of a happier time? If so she knew better, for her childhood had not been happy and the things it contained were best forgotten.

Leaning forward, heels drumming, she concentrated on the race. Beneath her she could feel the surge and pulse of muscle as her mount sent iron-shod hooves against the bare rock of the foothills. In her nostrils she could smell the odors of sweat and hair, of leather and oil, catch too the sensual scent of the beast; a mare close to seasonal heat—had that scent triggered her own femininity?

The drumming of the hooves softened as they hit a film of drifted soil; grains carried by the winds and trapped in the shelter of the cleft. Dull echoes rose to be caught and reflected by the soaring walls of either side. Before them shadows lay dense, sombre banks of thickening darkness which hid what lay beyond and seemed to hide the hint of movement.

Abruptly the mare came to a halt, raring, forelegs rising, eyes rolling, foam dropping from bared teeth and muzzle. A move which almost threw her, would have thrown her had she not been about to check the forward motion of the animal.

"Steady, girl! Steady!"

Charles, of course, had vanished, but she thought nothing of him as she ran her hands over the head and muzzle of the frightened beast, soothing the animal with words and touch. And the mare had reason to be afraid. She had ridden too long and wandered too far and now it was dangerously close to night. Looking up she saw the edges of the gulley framing a strip of purple sky palely flecked with the ghosts of stars. The suns were invisible, coming into view only when she had left the mountains and begun the journey home.

They were lower than she had thought and she cursed the delusia which had robbed her of elementary caution. Already the day was dying, the light diffused, the air holding a metallic taint, but with luck, she decided, she could just about make it. If it hadn't been for the stupid race with Charles she would have had no doubt but now, literally, it was a matter of life and death.

"Go!" She snapped to the mare. "Run for your life now, girl. Run!"

She helped, easing the stirrups, loosening the reins, placing her weight so as to help and not to hamper the rhythm of the animal. There was little more she could do. To have halted and removed the saddle would have lost time and the saving of weight was not as important as it would seem. The beast was accustomed to the saddle and she was not skilled in bare-backed riding.

"Move, girl! Move!"

It was no time to be gentle. The spurs she wore more for decoration than for actual use dug into the heaving flanks, the sting of the whip accentuating their message of urgency. Beneath her she felt the animal bound, fresh life sent to tiring muscles, the stride lengthening a little now they had reached flatter ground. Behind them the bulk of the mountains began to shrink as the ground streamed past around and below. The speed of their passage created a wind which thrummed against her face and caught her hair, tearing it free from the golden clasps which held it, fanning the thick, black tresses and sending them to stream like a silken pennant from the rounded contour of her head.

"On!" she urged. "On, girl! On!"

The sound of her voice acted as had the whip and spurs. Foam flew from the muzzle and the lungs strained in the barrel of the chest. A machine, bred and trained for strength, speed and obedience, the animal raced through the thickening darkness towards the haven which alone could save it. On its back the woman, sensing its fear and terror, conscious of her own, bit at her lower lip until blood stained her chin, the gleaming white perfection of her teeth.

Ellman's Rest, a gnarled and oddly shaped mass of wood and stone, the great tree surrounded by the rock which it had shattered by the relentless fury of its growth, appeared on

9

her right. Wisps of night-mist wreathed it, tattered veils which blurred detail so that for a moment she thought it was a creature of the unknown standing with outstretched arms to snatch her from the back of her mount, to crush her, to rend the limbs from her body and to tear free her internal organs. A moment of illusion, then the thing was behind and now only a few miles lay between her and the castle.

"We're winning," she said to the laboring animal. "Keep it up, girl. We're winning!"

The suns were behind her, the magenta and violet, their discs blended, now both below the horizon. Night was closing in, limiting her vision so that it was impossible to make out detail more than a few feet to either side, a little more ahead. Before her the trail wound like a snake, the narrow path curving between boulders, around looming mounds, straightening only to twist again. A bad road to take at speed even in the full light of day. One suicidal to attempt at a gallop on the edge of night.

"On, girl! On!"

The crest lay ahead, beyond it the curve, then the slope and, at last, a clear view of the castle. Once past the crest the road ran downhill and, beyond the curve, it was wide and evenly smooth. A place maintained for racing but never before had she raced with such determination to win. She would, she thought as they neared it, set a new record. Certainly it would be one which she never intended to break under similar circumstances.

Then, as something moved in the dimness, the animal shied.

There had been no warning, no intimation and, lulled by the nearing safety, she had relaxed a little. Too late she grabbed at the reins, felt the animal rear, and then was falling, hurtling through the air to land with a bone-jarring thud, her vision laced with darting flashes. As they cleared she rose and looked around. The animal had fallen and lay, screaming, on the dirt.

"It's hurt," said Charles. He stood at her side and looked at the stricken beast. "A broken leg, see?"

She didn't need the guidance of his pointing finger to discover the injury.

"Something frightened it. An animal of some kind crossing the trail." His voice was soft, even. "Nothing you need worry about. But the animal—you'll have to kill it."

The mare was young, healthy, a magnificent specimen of her species. She could be drugged, the leg mended with internal splints.

"You'll have to kill her," insisted Charles. "It's too dark to do anything else. You know that. You have no choice. At least be kind."

To the animal and then, perhaps, to herself. She looked around, shivering, feeling the skin crawl on her back and shoulders. The pull and drag of her loose tresses felt like hands tugging at her scalp. Their touch rasped dust and dirt over her tunic, little scraping sounds which, because near, rose above the screaming of the beast.

"Steady, girl!" She took small steps forward, talking, smiling as she spoke, one hand behind her, the fingers lifting the compact laser from her belt. "Steady, girl! Steady!"

The animal looked at her, eyes rolling, ears pricked, teeth bared in fright and pain. She stepped closer, kneeled beside the head, lifted the laser to rest its muzzle within the confines of an ear.

"Now," said Charles firmly. "Now!"

A click and it was done, the beam drilling through flesh and bone into the mass of the brain bringing quick and merciful peace.

Rising she looked down at the dead animal. It would be waiting for her and, should she follow it, they could ride again. As Charles would be waiting and so many others. A touch and it would be done.

"Lavinia! Lavinia, don't!"

She heard the shout and the thud of racing hooves, turned to see the dim figure in the dying light. Roland with a spare mount at his side.

"Up, girl!" he said urgently as he drew to a halt at her side. "Mount and ride!"

Delusia? The animals were real and Roland was alive as far as she knew. Quickly she mounted and felt the pound of hooves as the beast carried her down the road. Ahead loomed the bulk of the castle, the gates wide, closing as they

11

rode past them, slamming shut as the great curfew-bell sent throbbing echoes into the air.

"My lady, you are safe!" Old Giacomo, his face creased and seamed like the skin of a dried fruit, helped her to dismount. "The Old Ones heard my prayers!"

"And mine, my lady." A younger man, his son, she thought, touched a finger to his brow with due respect for her rank. Already he had presumed too far. "I also begged for the Old Ones to protect you."

"And I, my lady! And I!"

A sussuration, a chorus of voices, muttering, blending into a drone, turning words into things without meaning. For a moment she swayed, seeing the great courtyard filled with a great assembly, the host dotted with familiar faces. Fan de Turah, Ser M'tolah, Chun Chue, Tianark L'ouck—uncles and cousins and forebears whose portraits now hung in the galleries. Nobles who had come to stay and fight and die for the Family. Strangers whom she had never known but who now filled her castle. Generations which had lived and died before her own parents had been conceived.

"Lavinia!" Roland was at her side, his hand on her arm, his face anxious. "My dear, are you ill?"

"No."

"You look so pale." Gently he pushed back the thick strands of hair which had fallen over her cheek. "And your tunic is soiled. Did you fall?"

"Yes." She anticipated his concern. "It was nothing. Some bruises, perhaps, but nothing more."

"Even so a physician should examine you. Tomorrow I will send for one or, better, accompany you into town."

"No!" Always the tone of authority irritated her and yet she realized her sharpness had been uncalled for. He meant well and, of them all, he alone had ridden out for her. "No, Roland, she said more gently. "I'm not hurt. A hot bath and some massage is all I need."

He said, stiffly, "As you wish, my lady. I have no right to order, and yet I think you are being unwise."

"My lady?" She smiled and shook her head. "Roland you are my cousin and my friend. What need of such stiff formality? And where would I be now if you had not come to rescue me?"

A question he chose not to answer. Instead, as they walked from the courtyard towards the inner chambers, he said, "You were late, Lavinia. I was worried. What happened? Delusia?"

"Yes." She threw back her hair as they entered the corridor leading to her apartment. "Charles came to ride with me. He looked as I remembered him when we first met. Do you remember?"

"I was off world at the time," he said. "A business trip to Olmeyha."

"But you remember Charles, surely?"

"Yes." He looked down at his hands. They were thin, the knuckles prominent, the fingers too long for perfect symmetry. Only the nails, carefully polished and filed, revealed the fastidiousness of his nature. "Yes," he said again. "I remember him."

"The way he talked," she mused. "He opened doors for me which I didn't even know existed. The things he had done and intended to do. Had he lived I think I would have shared them."

"As the consort of an aging degenerate?" His tone was sharp, savagely dry. "Charles was older than you suspected, Lavinia. You were young then, little more than a child, trusting, impressionable, a little—"

"Foolish?"

"I didn't say that."

"But you meant it." Anger glowed in her eyes and turned the dark orbs into pools of smouldering fire. "Is that what you think of me?"

"No. Lavinia, don't jump to conclusions."

"Young," she said. "Little more than a child. Trusting. Impressionable. Well, perhaps all that is true, even though I was more than a child. But foolish? No. Not unless it is foolish to ache to learn. Stupid to want to be a woman. Do you still think I was a fool?"

"To be charmed by Charles, yes." Stubbornly he refused to yield. "I knew him, perhaps not too well, but better than you did. He was a lecher, a gambler, a degenerate. Think, girl, it was written on his face. You saw him at the last."

"He'd been ill!"

"Yes." Roland looked again at his hands. "Yes, he'd been ill."

Wasting from the effects of a corrosive poison fed to him by an outraged husband, but what need to explain that? The girl was enamored of a dream, the slave to memory.

She said, gently, "Roland, my friend, we have been quarreling and that is wrong. I owe you my life. Between us should be nothing but harmony. If I have offended you I beg your forgiveness. You will give it?"

He took her extended hands into his own, feeling their soft firmness, their grace, their warmth. Tilting his head he looked into her eyes, deep-set under high-arched brows, studying the glow of light reflected from her cheekbones, the line of her jaw. The mouth was full, the lower lip, swollen from the impact of her teeth, a ruby pout. Her ears were small and tight against the curve of her skull. The hair, dishevelled now, was an ebon mane streaked with a band of silver.

"My lady!" He stooped so as to hide the worship in his eyes.

"Roland!" Her hands freed themselves from his grasp, one touching his hair, running over the thinning strands. "My friend! My very good friend!"

"Lavinia!"

"I must bathe and change." She turned from him, seeing a figure standing beside her door, waiting. "We shall meet again at dinner. And, Roland, once again my thanks."

Charles accompanied her through the portal and stood watching as she stripped. The bath was hot, the scented water easing aches and pains, a cloud of steam rising to dim the lines of the chamber, the figure of her maid.

"A dreadful thing, my lady," she said. She had heard the news as servants always did. Often Lavinia had wondered just how they knew all that was going on. "To think of you being shut outside! Lord Acrae insisted the curfew shouldn't be rung until he'd brought you safe inside and he set men to enforce his orders. But what if something had happened, my lady? Suppose his mount had fallen? What if night had fallen before you were back inside?"

"If you had wings, girl, you'd be a bird."

"My lady?"

"Forget it." It was cruel to talk in ways the girl couldn't

14

understand. "True night falls when the curfew is sounded," she explained. "Or, to put it another way, only when the curfew bell is rung has true night fallen. Do you understand?"

"I—I think so, my lady."

She didn't and Lavinia waved her away. She was too ignorant to understand the subtle difference between night falling and a bell sounding the falling of night. A bell could be delayed and Roland had done just that. He had been shrewder than she'd known. The difference could only have been in minutes, perhaps, but those minutes would or could have made all the difference. At least the Pact had not been obviously flaunted and the Sungari had no grounds for complaint.

"Charles?" She looked through the drifting steam but the figure had vanished. Delusia had passed. It would return but she missed him.

Would they have married had he lived?

Lying in the steaming, scented water she ran her hands over the curves and silken skin of her body. It was a good one, she knew, even though not as young as once it had been. The time for marriage had come and gone with her father failing in his duty, her uncle more concerned with his own affairs, her mother turning to the past and finally swallowing poison to be with the object of an early passion.

Alone she had worked to maintain the Family estates, the castle, the house in town. Retainers needed money for food and clothing, doweries had to be provided for the female servants, homes and work for the men. Some of the young had become restless and had left to move on and try their luck on other worlds. There had been friction with the Sungari, the Pact barely maintained and lost crops had created hardship. And now Lord Gydapen was turning difficult.

"My lady?" The maid was at the edge of the bath. "Are you ready for your massage now?"

"Later."

"But soon it will be time for dinner and your hair needs to be dressed and—"

"Later." Lavinia stretched, guessing the girl had a lover waiting, not caring if she had. Let the fellow wait, he would appreciate the girl all the more for having his pleasure delayed. And he, the girl also, must learn that, above all, her wishes were paramount. "Later, I said. Argue and I'll have you whipped!"

It was harder to relax this time, the irritation lingered. Gydapen and the irritation, a good combination, one giving rise to the other. Perhaps she should encourage his attentions? His estates were to the south, rich lands providing a fat harvest, a gain for her and food for her people. A marriage would be politically wise if otherwise distasteful. Rich he might be but Gydapen was lacking in certain attributes which would have claimed her attention. His height for one; how could she bear to look down on her consort? His girth could be lessened and his age was no real handicap; the extra years would hasten his natural end. Love, of course, did not enter into it.

Could she bear to marry without love? To allow a man to touch her body as she touched it now? To use her, to breed children in her belly, to make her a thing of his own?

She knew the answer even as she turned in the water, restless, conscious of her needs, the demands of her flesh aroused by the thoughts of desire. If a sacrifice had to be made for the Family then she would make it. If Gydapen could provide peace and security and demanded her body as the price then she would pay it.

But it would be nice to marry for love.

Lying in the water, eyes half-closed, drifting in an ocean of erotic fantasies, she thought about it. A man who would come into her life as Charles had done, sweeping her off her feet, overwhelming her with his masculinity. A man of culture and sophistication, gentle and yet knowing when to be cruel, masterful and yet knowing when to yield. A man she could trust to stand at her side. A father for her children. A lover to be enjoyed.

A dream to be enjoyed as the bath was to be enjoyed. A self-indulgence which must remain limited to a brief duration. Her maid could hope for such a man, every servant in the castle, every daughter of a minor noble, but she stood alone. And, even if she was free to choose, where on all Zakym could such a man be found?

Chapter TWO

The guard was neatly uniformed in scarlet and emerald; bright colors which made him conspicuous but which did nothing to reduce his dignity. A man of middle-age, his face round and unsmiling, his voice was firmly polite.

"All persons arriving on Harald are required to deposit the cost of a High passage with the authorities. Exceptions, of course, are made for residents and for those travelling on inclusive tours arranged by reputable companies. Do you fall into either of the latter categories, sir?"

Dumarest said, flatly, "You know the answer to that. No."

"Then I must ask you for the deposit. A receipt will be issued, naturally, and you can claim repayment on departure."

"And if I haven't got it?"

The guard shrugged. "You could, perhaps, arrange for a passage to another world. If you lack even the money for that then you will be confined to a special area. Those with work to offer will seek you out. In time, with luck, you could gain enough to move on."

A lot of time and even more luck. The stranded would have no chance of breaking free of the trap. Those offering work would pay only minimal rates and what money earned would go on food. It would be impossible ever to gain the price of a High passage. Even if a man managed to get enough to travel Low, riding doped, frozen and ninety per cent dead in a casket designed for the transportation of animals, the odds were against him. Starved, emaciated, such a journey would be certain death. Only the fit could hope to survive and even they ran the risk of the fifteen per cent death rate.

Dumarest said, dryly, "Usually when a man is stranded on a planet he has the chance of making his own way. Why the compound?"

"Desperate men are dangerous. Harald is a civilized world. We want no man-shaped animals hunting in our streets."

"And no paupers, either?"

"And no paupers." The guard looked over his shoulder towards the town. It seemed a nice place, tall buildings of at least a dozen stories rising above the painted roofs of sprawling dwellings. Even the field was well laid out, the perimeter fence tall and ringed with lights, the warehouses set in neat array. The compound, Dumarest guessed, would be placed well away from the public eye.

Lowtowns usually were.

"You have the deposit?" The guard was growing impatient even though his tone remained polite. Old enough to have learned caution he knew that a harsh and brusk manner would gain him nothing except, perhaps, a knife in the throat. And Dumarest looked the type of man who knew how to handle a knife.

"I have it." Dumarest counted out the money, thick coins issued by the Jarmasin-Pontianak Combine and recognized on a hundred worlds. He frowned as the guard held out a pad. "What's this for?"

"Your thumbprint. It's for your own protection," the guard explained. "A receipt can get lost or be stolen but no one can steal your thumbprint. The right hand and rest the ball within the square. Your name?" He wrote it down, apparently unaware of the momentary hesitation. "Thank you, sir. I hope you enjoy your stay."

"Is there any limit as to duration?"

"None." Now that the formalities had been seen to the guard was willing to talk. "Of course, should you run into

18

debt, become a public charge or show criminal tendencies action will be taken. As I said we have a nicely civilized world here and we want to maintain our standards. If you run into trouble your deposit will be on hand to ship you out if the need arises. We don't believe in hurting ourselves to keep the useless." Deftly he changed the subject. "Are you here for any special purpose?"

"To look around. To work, maybe. There is work?"

"Plenty. You'll find details at the agency. If you want a hotel I'd recommend the Wanderer's Rest. It's a nice place, clean and not too expensive. My wife's sister runs it. Tell her I sent you and she'll do her best."

"I'll think about it," said Dumarest.

"You do that."

"I will."

That and other things. His name and thumbprint registered at the gate, both obviously to be fed into a computer, a record impossible for him to erase and a signpost to any who might be looking. And some would be looking, of that he was sure. A mistake to have paid the deposit, perhaps, another way could have been found, but it would have taken time and needless risk. Speed then, he decided. He would do what he had come to do and do it fast.

Dumarest slowed and looked around. A wide road ran from the field now busy with traffic and pedestrians. Men and women, neatly dressed, their faces telling of comfortable living, wandered on either side. Shops with large windows of glass or transparent plastic offered a variety of goods for sale. Taverns echoed soft music and the scents of food.

A nice, warm, comfortable world and Dumarest could understand the desire of the inhabitants to keep it that way.

A car slowed to halt beside him, the driver, a young man with a peaked cap adorned with multi-colored piping smiling from his seat.

"Want to ride, mister?"

"No."

"I'm heading into the city. Half a deci gets you there. A cut-rate, mister, and why hurt yourself for a little money?" His smile widened as Dumarest sat in the passenger compartment. "Anywhere special?"

"You know the Wanderer's Rest?"

"Sure." Eyes too old for the face slid towards him. "It's a home for the senile. You want a little action then leave it to me. Some luxuries, maybe? A girl or two? Some gambling? Name it and it's yours."

"Just take me where I said."

Leaning back Dumarest studied the town. The buildings were all in good repair but with a pool of cheap labor readily available that was to be expected. As was the absence of beggars and the usual touts to be found at any landing field, but the driver had already said enough for him to know that what he saw was a facade over the usual vice.

"Right, mister." The driver held out a hand. "The Wanderer's Rest. Two decis."

"You said a half."

"Man, you're crazy. The fare is two. You want to argue I'll call a guard."

Dumarest looked to either side. Down the street he caught a flash of scarlet and emerald. Opposite a pair of women were gossiping and, lower down, a young couple walked arm in arm.

"Two decis." The driver snapped his fingers. "Come on, man, give. I've no time to haggle with a yokel."

"Two decis," said Dumarest. He fumbled in a pocket, leaning close, hiding the driver from view. The man squealed as fingers closed like steel claws around his arm. "Is a broken arm worth it?"

"You! I—" The man gulped as fingers dug into flesh and grated against bone. "No, mister! No!"

"Two decis?"

Sweat beaded the driver's face as he stared into the hard visage inches from his eyes. The hand gripping his arm was threatening to tear the muscle from the bone, to snap the limb. The pain of impacted nerves was a fire searing naked tissue.

"No! A mistake! For God's sake, mister, let me go!"

"To shout for the guard? To argue about the fare?"

"No!"

"Changed your mind about cheating me?" Dumarest climbed back into the vehicle. "Drop me in the middle of town."

It ringed a plaza set with fountains and flowering shrubs,

shaded by graceful trees and dotted with convenient benches. Some children played at the foot of a statue; a cluster of men with their faces turned upwards to face the sky. It had been cast from a reddish metal now bright and smoothly polished. A man stood before it a duster in his hand. He was dressed in grey, wore a round hat and had a wide collar of dull, black metal clamped around his neck.

Dumarest said, "How much do they pay you?"

"Pay me?" The man turned, blinking. "Who are you, mister? Why do you ask?"

"I'm curious. Well?"

"I don't get paid," said the man, dully. "But for each day I work I get five decis knocked off my debt."

And, if he tried to run, the radio-linked collar could be activated to blow the head from his shoulders.

"What about your deposit?"

"What deposit? I was born here." The man turned to wipe his duster over the statue. "At that I'm lucky. They won't let me starve and I'm given shelter. My wife left me, of course, and my kid disowned me but, in seven years, three months and eleven days they'll unlock this collar and set me free."

"And, if someone paid the debt?"

"I'd be freed at once. I only owed money, mister, I didn't hurt anyone. Even if I had I could buy my way out after taking my lashes. You—no."

"Something?"

"You look like a stranger. If you want some good advice get off this world as soon as you can. Without money you'd be better off dead and, if you've got some, they'll be after it. The vultures, I mean. But who the hell ever takes good advice?"

"I do." Dumarest handed the man twenty days of freedom. "This isn't charity—I don't believe in it. I'm buying information. Where can I find the best computer service in town?"

It was housed in an ornate building which reared close to the edge of the city. Glass reflected the light of the setting sun as Dumarest made his way towards it and he paused, looking at the intricate stone-work, wondering who had paid for it and why.

Inside he found out. The receptionist was svelte, young,

vaguely interested in his requirements. A woman, he guessed, with more than work on her mind. Patiently he explained his needs.

"Computer time, certainly, that's what we're here to deliver. Now if you will let us have the relevant documents and authorization—"

"What authorization?"

"Why, the permission to use the documents for the purpose your claim." Long eyelashes dropped to cover impatient eyes. "Is it really necessary for me to explain?"

Dumarest said, coldly, "I am a personal friend of the Director. He has asked me to conduct a test of your attitude towards the general public. I find it most interesting. Now, if you please, I would like your name and status." His tone chilled even more. "At once!"

"I— But you can't! I mean—"

"You deny me the information? Am I to assume you lack the right to sit where you do? Inform your superior that I wish to make an immediate appointment. Move, girl. Move!"

Twenty minutes later he was ushered into an office occupying the corner of the fifth floor. A woman rose as he entered, coming forward to meet him, both hands extended. As their palms touched she said, "Earl Dumarest. You have been on this world less than two hours and already I have one slightly hysterical girl on my hands. Are you really a friend of the Director?"

A woman who knew so much would know more. "No."

"I am glad that you didn't lie. It would have been a stupid pretence. My name, incidentally is Hilda Benson. My status, if you are interested, is comptroller of external outlets." She smiled, a dumpy, aging woman who radiated an air of competence. "What made you so annoyed downstairs?"

"Stupidity."

"The girl's or the system's?"

"Perhaps both. She wanted documents—I have none. She demanded an authorization to use the documents I didn't have. We were getting nowhere."

"So you did something about it. Please sit. Now, how can we help you?" She frowned as he told her. "You want to find a world? A planet called Earth? And you come to us for that?"

"Where better?"

"An almanac, surely. One can be found in any library."

"Can you supply the information?"

"Of course. If a library has the information then so do we. An incredible amount of data is stacked in our memory banks and that information naturally includes all known astronomical data, all navigational tables, the most recent listing and—" She broke off, shaking her head. "Well, it's your money and if you want to waste it who am I to object? Earth, you say?" A terminal stood to one side of the office and she crossed to it, her fingers dancing over the keys. "This will only take a moment."

Dumarest leaned back in the chair, waiting. After a while he said, "Is something wrong?"

"No." She looked a little flustered. "It's just that we have to wait our turn. I'll ask again and demand priority."

"The response will be—planet unknown," said Dumarest. "Am I correct?"

"You are." She looked at him from her position by the terminal. "Which means that the world you mention does not exist."

"Because your computer does not hold the information?" He shrugged. "Try again, madam. Ask under 'legends.' Also under the name 'Terra.' And if you have anything on the Original People it might help."

"Is this a joke?"

"No." He met her eyes. "I came here for help not to make a fool of anyone. I understand that the computers on Harald are the finest in the entire region. I take it they are cross-linked?" He paused, continuing at her nod, "All that remains then is to select the finest service. I was given to understand that this was it. Maybe you're more interested in fancy decoration and prestige-buildings than in actual service."

"You don't have to be insulting."

"I don't have to be anything!" Dumarest surged to his feet. "Certainly I don't have to beg for what I pay for or plead for what you are in business to provide. Now hit those keys and let's find out just how damned good your computers are."

For a long moment she stood, looking at him, her eyes searching his face and then, as if having arrived at a decision, turned to the terminal and sent her blunt fingers over the keys.

He heard the hiss of her indrawn breath as she read the answer flashed on the screen.

"Well?"

"Legend," she said. "It's listed under legend. Earth is a mythical world—"

"Wrong!"

"—one equated with Eden, Avalon, Camelot, El Dorado, Jackpot, Bonanza and many others," she continued, ignoring the interruption. "One of a group of tales possibly devised to entertain children or to point a moral. A fable of a place devoid of hurt, pain or sorrow."

"Wrong again," he said, harshly. "Earth has all of those and more. Try again."

"Terra?"

"Another name for Earth." He waited as she operated the keyboard. "Well?"

"As you say, it is another name for Earth, but I've something from the Original People. You would, no doubt, like to tell me what it is."

He smiled at the acidity of her tone; an expression without genuine humor, but one which helped. There was no point in making her an enemy.

"The Original People are a cult which believe that all men sprang from a single world. I quote—" his voice deepened, held something of the muted thunder of drums, "From terror they fled to find new places on which to expiate their sins. Only when cleansed will the race of Man be again united." As she drew in her breath he said, "End of quote. Good enough?"

"For me, yes. You know what you're talking about and I don't think you are joking. But you realize what you're asking us to do?"

"To find the coordinates of Earth."

"To find a legend. A place which officially doesn't exist. Do you realize what that could mean? Endless checking of cross-references, the hunting down of abstruse notations, the searching of ancient files. Elimination, selection, winnowing, collating, substantiating—it could take years! She saw his expression. "You disagree?"

"Not with what you say. Such a search would take a long time and there would be no certainty of success. But I don't want you to do that. I merely want to hire the computer to run a comparison check on a stellar spectrogram I have. How much would it cost?"

"We charge by the minute." He pursed his lips as she told him the price. "Are you still interested?"

"How long would it take?"

She said, precisely, "There are over a half billion stars registered in the memory banks. Some elimination is possible, naturally, but even so it will take time. And first the input information must be prepared. You have the data?"

She took the strip of film he handed to her, a copy of the one he had found on Emijar and, holding it, said, "There will be an initial fee of two hundred. This will cover breakdown and isolation of relevant identifying aspects. The material will, naturally, be yours."

"Two hundred decis?"

"Mettres."

Ten times as much—no wonder they had graced the building with expensive carvings. Twice the cost of a Low passage but worth it if he could gain the coordinates.

She said, as if reading his mind, "You realize this is only the initial payment. The fee for computer hire will be extra."

A hundred a minute and he'd thought she'd meant decis. Now he knew better. Harald, it seemed, was an expensive world in more ways than one.

"Have you any idea how long it could take?"

"The computer can check ten thousand bits every second. Assuming the entire half billion has to be checked it is a matter of simple division. Ten thousand into five hundred million divided by sixty to obtain minutes, multiplied by a hundred comes to—" she paused a moment, frowning, "Say about eighty-three thousand. The average should be half of that, say forty-two thousand. Of course, we could hit the answer within the first second."

"And that would cost only a hundred?"

"No." Gently she shook her head. "For an investigation like this we should require a deposit of ten thousand minimum. That, of course, will buy you a hundred minutes and you could be lucky."

"And if not?"

"Then we'd freeze the program until you had handed us more. It would be best to arrange for a complete run and take a gamble. I could arrange it for forty-five thousand and you would be certain of a complete check. If we run over the half-way mark, of course, we stand to lose."

"How?" He spoke before she could answer. "I know—the extra running time would be for free. Supposing I paid just what would I get?"

"The answer if it is to be found. A complete check of all comparisons made in any case—information which would be valuable in itself. For elimination purposes," she explained. "It is remotely possible that some other computer has information on stars which we lack. The data we would give you could isolate those stars and possibly supply the missing item." For a moment she was silent then, quietly said, Well?"

If he'd had the money he would have told her to go ahead—what was money when compared to finding Earth? But he didn't have it and nothing like it. The two hundred, yes, but what good would be the initial preparation data?

"Could I leave it for now?"

"Of course." She handed him back the strip of film. Reaching for it their fingers met and she froze at the contact, sensing something of the disappointment which filled him. "Look," she said with sudden generosity. "There is nothing I can do to help you. I work for the company and you must understand why. But there is a man, a hobbyist in a way, and he might be able to do something. I'll give you his name and address." She scribbled on a pad. "Be gentle with him, please. Once we were friends."

Once long ago perhaps, but now he had found another. One which came in convenient containers and held the old, insidious charm. Dumarest stared at the man who opened the door and recognized the traces on face and bearing. Smelt too the sickly odor of the habitual drunk.

"Armand Ramhed?"

"The same. And you?" Armand craned forward, blinking. Tall, his head came level with Dumarest's own but his bulk was only half as much. His skin was creped, mottled, sagging in tiny pouches. His watery eyes were bagged and his throat resembled the scrawny limb of a starved bird. "Who are you, sir?" He blinked again as Dumarest gave his name and that of the woman who had sent him. Now he knew why she had asked him to be gentle.

"Hilda?" Armand smiled with genuine pleasure. "A wonderful woman, sir, and a true friend. Come in. Come in. Anything I can do to help I will do. For her I can do no less."

Inside the house was surprisingly clean though thinly furnished. Some bottles stood against a wall, all empty. Another stood on a table together with a glass. From the rear came the stench of fermenting fluids.

"You will drink with me?" Armand, without waiting for an answer, found a second glass. It was thick, smeared, the edge chipped a little. "It is only home-brew but it has some merit. A good body and the flavor, though I say it myself, is rewarding to those of discernment. A trifle young, of course, but there, we can't have everything can we? To your very good health, sir."

Dumarest watched as he swallowed the contents of his glass then took a sip of his own. He was pleasantly surprised. The wine, though a little rough, did hold the body Armand had claimed and the flavor, while strange, was not repulsive. And it was strong.

"You like it?" Like a child the man was eager for praise but there was no need to lie.

"I've drunk worse on a score of worlds," said Dumarest. "And been on as many more where a bottle of this would fetch a full mettre." Deliberately he emptied his glass.

"Some more?"

"Later." Dumarest produced the strip of film. "Hilda said that perhaps you could help me. If you can it will be worth some money."

"Is friendship to be bought?"

"No, but service is to be paid for." Dumarest explained the problem. "What can you do?"

"Perhaps nothing." Armand squinted at the film. "This

needs to be magnified and projected—come into the other room."

It was a crude laboratory, a mess of varigated equipment strewn over a table and the floor, wires running from rough assemblies, hand-made mechanisms to all sides.

"Sit," ordered Armand. "Help yourself to drink if you want, but don't disturb me. This will take some time."

Time to sit and think and plant a little. Time to appreciate the irony of the situation and taste the bitter gall of defeat. He had, Dumarest was certain, the long-sought key to the whereabouts of the world he had searched to find for so long. Over the years he had gathered a handful of clues; a name, a sector, a mnemonic, some distances and names of nearby stars and then, finally, the one sure means to identify the primary from all others. The spectrogram he had found; the lost treasure of a forgotten cult.

It held the answer, he was sure of it. It would tell him what he wanted to know. Information which would yield the essential coordinates and put an end to the bitter search. The answer at last—all he needed was the money to pay for it.

Chapter THREE

Armand Ramhed lived alone in a house which held little more than a bed, a table, a few chairs, some kitchen equipment and the apparatus he had assembled in his study. Dumarest roved through it, checking the contents of the cupboards and finding nothing but empty packets and scraps of mouldering food. The air in the kitchen stank of the fermenting liquid; a thick slime coated with a yellow crust ornamented with a shimmer of bursting bubbles. It contained a mixture of fruits, vegetables, sugars and traces of acids, syrups and crushed roots. Garbage, Dumarest guessed, collected from the market place, pounded, boiled, diluted, used as food by the yeasts which clouded it, their waste the alcohol which had come to dominate Armand's life.

The man waved an irritable hand as Dumarest entered his study.

"Go away, Earl. Don't interrupt me. I haven't finished yet."

"It's late."

"Is it?" Armand lifted his head, blinking. The windows were shuttered, the only light that coming from the crude apparatus over which he crouched. Colored beams streamed

29

from it to paint his face with a rainbow. In the illumination his thin features took on the grotesque appearance of a clown. "I hadn't noticed. How late is it?"

"It's dark. Are you hungry?" Dumarest had expected the shake of the head. Alcohol, especially when loaded with organic particles, could feed as well as numb. "Well, I am. You've nothing to eat in the house. Where's the nearest store?"

It lay down the road, a small automat which swallowed coins and disgorged pre-packed items. Dumarest returned loaded with a package stuffed with basic commodities together with more perishable viands. An hour later he dragged Armand from his study and sat him at the table.

"Earl, this is a waste. I'm not hungry. I'm—" The man broke off, sniffing. "Meat? Is that meat?"

It was steak, thick and rare, served with three kinds of vegetable, flavored and rich in spiced oils. As Armand stared at it Dumarest said, shortly, "Eat."

"But—"

"Eat." He set an example, cutting, lifting slivers of meat to his mouth. "Take your time, chew it well, but eat."

The food had little obvious effect, it would take a month of such feeding to even begin to plump out the sunken cheeks, but a trace of color graced the shallow flesh and the eyes held a sharper directness than before.

"That was good." Armand sighed as he wiped oil from his mouth. "You certainly know how to cook, Earl. But then you would, wouldn't you?"

"Why?"

"A traveller has to be the master of many skills. To hunt, trap, butcher, cook—without that ability how to survive? And to eat when food is available because there can never be any certainty of when the next meal will offer the chance to eat again. You see? I know a little about such things."

"You've travelled?"

"A little when young. It is a disease of youth, is it not? The urge to be up and moving, to see new worlds, new places. To find adventure and excitement and, perhaps, romance. Well, I found no treasure and no rich women waiting to fall into my arms. I was offered no exotic employment and found no natural advantage. But some things I did find."

"Dirt," said Dumarest softly. "Discomfort. Pain and hunger. Cold indifference, men who cheated, women who lied. Poverty and what it can bring."

"The need to be utterly selfish," whispered Armand. "To be greedy, to give nothing away which could be sold, to concentrate every thought and action on the need to survive. And the loneliness. The loneliness."

"So you returned to Harald?"

"After a couple of years, yes. I'd made a friend, together we travelled Low, but when we landed he had died in transit. It decided things for me. Some men are not made in an adventurer's mold. So I came back home and took up a post with—well, never mind. And then—but that doesn't matter now either."

"Perhaps one thing does."

"Hilda?" Armand looked bleakly at his hands. "It's too late for that now. Once we could have made a life together but I was weak while she was strong. Weak!" His fist slammed against the table. "The story of my life. Always I have been weak. Earl!"

He needed his demon and it would do little harm on top of such richly oiled food. And his metabolism, accustomed to alcohol, would be demanding. Silently Dumarest handed the man a glass, watched as he plunged it into the bubbling vat. A gulp and it was empty.

"How are you progressing?"

"On the spectrogram?" Armand helped himself to another drink. "Slowly. The work is engrossing and a puzzle of interest but there are so many variables to take into account before it will be possible to present a final picture."

"Just what are you trying to do?"

"Nothing a computer couldn't do if correctly programmed. Basically, by a process of elimination, I'm saving you money. You want to find a certain star, right? But stars are not all the same. There are blue-violets, red giants, white dwarfs, variables, binaries, stars rich in radio waves, others verging on neutronic collapse."

"So?"

"I have determined that your spectrogram belongs to a G-type star, one of medium size, fairly stable, past the first flush of its creation but far from age-collapse. This alone, as you can see, is a great saving. A hired computer can be programmed to make comparisons only with stars of a similar type.

Dumarest said, grimly, "Did the woman lie to me? She said—"

"What, in her position, she had to say. The company does not exist to teach its customers how to save money. If you asked for a complete comparison check then that is what you would have been given." Armand shrugged. "Come, Earl, did you expect them to be charitable?"

On Harald nothing could be charitable. Dumarest said, "So you've isolated the spectral type. Good. What remains? A simple check?"

"Not so simple." Armand sipped at his drink and shrugged at Dumarest's expression. "You think that all we need to do is to expand the spectrum, isolate and determine the thickness and density of the Fraunhofer lines and then, as soon as we have found a match, there is the answer. Is that so?"

"What else?"

"The red shift." Armand lifted his glass, saw Dumarest's eyes and hastily placed it down. "Stars are at varying distances," he explained. "Any spectogram taken from one point will serve to identify all stars as seen from that point. Good enough—but what happens if we take a spectrogram of the same star but from different distances? They would have to be great, naturally, but only relatively so. And the direction too, that can have a bearing."

"The Doppler Effect," said Dumarest. "If the light comes from a source moving towards you it moved towards the blue end of the spectrum. If from a source moving away then it shifts towards the red."

"Exactly, and so we get the name for the phenomena." Armand frowned, thoughtful. "But why call it that? Why not the blue shift or the red-blue shift? You called it what— the Doppler Effect?"

"A name given to it by an old scientist I once knew. He learned it from an old book." Dumarest dismissed the matter of terminology with an impatient gesture. "Never mind what we call it, what effect does it have as far as I'm concerned?"

"It introduces a variable. If your spectrogram was taken

from a point close to the primary it will be minutely different from those taken at great distances and they, in turn, will differ from each other depending on which position relative to the source they were taken. You see the difficulty?"

Find Earth and he would be able to identify Earth's sun—but his only interest in the primary was as a guide to the planet itself. A vicious circle—or was it?

"No." Boldly Armand took another drink. "I mentioned it to illustrate the difficulties but the real answer lies in the Fraunhofer lines. What I am doing is to isolate them, determine their position and density, correlate them with the elements which gave them birth and so build up a pattern stripped of all unessentials. Once I have done that a computer-comparison will be relatively cheap." He anticipated Dumarest's question. "At a rough guess I'd say in the region of a fifth to a tenth. It would depend, of course, on the company."

"Of course," said Dumarest, and clamped his hand on the other's wrist as he again made to lift his glass. "You'd better get back to work, yes?"

"And you?"

"I'm going to look around town."

The night had come with a thin scatter of rain and it puddled the streets, gleaming on the sidewalks, rising in pluming fountains from beneath the wheels of passing traffic. It was close to midnight, the area around the house dark with shuttered windows, sparse overhead lights throwing patches of brightness interspersed with pools of shadow.

A quiet, safe place by the look of it, but if it were it would be the first Dumarest had seen. Already he knew that the old vices ruled beneath the surface but here was not the place to look for what he wanted to find. Closer to the field he found it.

"Mister!" The voice whispered from a shadowed doorway. "You lost?"

"No, just looking."

"For a little fun?" His clothing had told the woman he was a stranger. The tunic with its high collar and long sleeves held tight at the wrists together with pants of matching grey plastic tucked into knee-high boots were the mark of a traveller. Such a man could be lonely.

"I could help out, maybe." She stepped into the light, tilting her head so as to look into his face. Her body sagged beneath the faded clothing she wore and her face was lost beneath a mask of paint. Only the eyes were alive, hard, questing. "I've a place nearby. Music, wine, some food if you want. I'm a good cook."

"No thanks."

"Not hungry?" She wasn't talking about food. "I've a spice which will take care of that. Something to get you in the mood and keep you in it for as long as you want. And I won't skin you, mister. We'll make a fair deal." Her eyes searched his face. "No? Something else then?"

Dumarest handed her coins. "If I wanted to watch some fights where would I go?"

"Fights?" Her tone sharpened. "You mean with knives?"

"Yes."

"You fooled me, mister. You don't look like a degenerate. Is that the way you get your kicks? Watching kids slash each other to ribbons? Betting, maybe? God, at times you men make me sick." Then, as he stood waiting, she added, "Try Benny at the Novator. It's down the road to the right of the gate as you come out."

The place was as Dumarest expected and similar to others he had known. A room with girls serving drinks. Food on a counter. Music from concealed speakers and the lights turned low so as to shield the faces of those who sat huddled in cubicles. But the whole thing was a facade. Behind lay the ring, the tiered seats, the lights, the stench of sweat and oil and blood.

The arena!

Always they were to be found, the places where men and women vented their primitive lust for blood, taking a vicarious pleasure from another's victories, gloating at another's pain. An escape some called it, a release from accumulated pressures. A few spoke of it as a therapy, a means to cool the aggressive instincts, to govern the beast which lurked always beneath the skin. Others called it butchery.

To Benny it was a business.

"You're lucky," he said to Dumarest. "We've started but

there are still a couple of seats going. The first tier—the best."

And the highest priced, but Dumarest handed over the tariff without argument. To him, too, the arena was a business and he had come, not to gloat, but to study.

"Kill!" screamed a woman as he took his seat. "Kill, the bastard!" Kill!"

She was a middle-aged matron, normally poised, normally horrified at the prospect of violence, but now the madness of the place had gripped her and she looked barely human.

As the others around her had changed, screaming for one man to kill another, to cut him open, to spill his blood, to act the butcher for their entertainment.

Their favorite did his best to oblige.

He was a tall, thin man with a scarred face and a torso thick with scars. A dancer who stood poised on the balls of his feet, always moving, never still, the ten-inch blade in his hand catching and reflecting the light in a constant shimmer of splintered brightness. A swift, hard, dangerous man. One who had learned his trade the hard way and bore the stigmata of previous failures in the cicatrices which patterned his body. A man who intended to earn his fee and the bonus of coins which would shower from the crowd if he pleased them.

His opponent was younger, as fast but not as skilled, a novice and hopelessly out of his class, matched for use as a victim more than anything else. Blood ran from a shallow gash on one shoulder, more from a minor cut on his left forearm. A thrust, barely missed, had ripped the top of his shorts so that threads hung in a ragged bunch. Sweat made them limp. Sweat ran over the face and body, oozing beneath the oil. Dumarest could smell his fear.

"Kill him!" screamed the woman at his side. "Kill!"

The tall fighter turned, smiling, lifting his knife in salute. A move which left him open; an apparent carelessness which the younger man was quick to put to his advantage. He came in, knife gripped like a sword, the point slightly raised, the edge turned inwards. So held the blade was ready to stab, to cut, to block, to turn and slash.

He almost made it—or so the tall man made it seem. As the attack developed he jumped back, appeared to stumble, moved clumsily to one side as the keen steel whined through the air where he had stood. A slash delivered too late and with too much effort. Unopposed the force put into it turned the younger man too far to his left. His recovery was too slow and a yell rose from the crowd as a third wound marked his gleaming flesh. A long cut running over the pectoral muscles of his chest.

A cut which had severed muscle, released blood, created pain.

The first of those which would leave him a maimed and crippled thing.

"Galbrio!" screamed the matron. "You did it! You did it!" Tearing a ring from her finger she threw it into the ring. "My hero! My love!"

The offer was in her voice, her eyes. Should he care to take her, she was his for as long as the stimulated passion which now controlled her should last. Then, after it had died, she would go home, satiated, a little disturbed, swearing, perhaps, never to witness another fight, but the vow would be broken and the ritual again experienced.

Like an addictive drug the spectacle of blood and pain was hard to relinquish.

Dumarest rose as the shouting died. Dropping to the sunken level surrounding the ring he made his way to the dressing rooms. There were small, cubicles holding the personal effects of those who fought, a few private chambers for the prime contenders, an open area fitted with a blood-stained table on which the hurt were given crude first aid. To one side rested the boxes for the dead.

Benny sat on the pile of coffins. He held a pomander in one hand and sniffed it as he looked at the screaming wretch now on the table. As Dumarest touched his arm he turned with a cat-like swiftness.

"What—oh, it's you! What do you want?"

"A chance at Galbrio."

"You want to fight him?" Benny began to shake his head, halting the gesture as he ran his eyes over Dumarest's face. "Hell, you made it. But why? The man's good. The best. He'd butcher you inside three minutes."

"Maybe."

"He would. I know him. Do you?"

His type only, but it was enough. Cold, ruthless, devoid of mercy, the way a good fighter should be. But he had a streak of cruelty, a sadistic pleasure in inflicting pain. The young man had been maimed with savage deliberation. The wounds had cut too deep and had been wrongly placed simply to please the crowd. There had been a spiteful intent behind the act and, as Dumarest knew, the man's days were numbered.

"I'll make it simple," he said. "First blood or third; to the death or a timed end; a split purse or winner take all." He let his voice falter a little. "I don't care. I just don't care."

"You in trouble?" Benny guessed the answer. "Need cash bad, uh? Is that why you come here?" He beamed at Dumarest's silence. "I can fit you in but the purse will be small. Hell, what else do you expect? An unknown."

"Set a purse," said Dumarest. "Winner take all. And I'll back myself against Galbrio."

"Galbrio? Maybe he won't want to know."

But he did as Dumarest had known he would. An apparent novice willing to put himself at the mercy of his blade. Another victim to throw to the crowd, more cash and jewelry thrown into the ring, an easy victory and a cheap enhancing of his reputation. No man with his inclinations could miss the opportunity.

Only when they stripped did he sense that, perhaps, he had made a mistake.

"You've fought before," he said, looking at the thin lines of old scars on Dumarest's chest and forearms. "Often?"

"Only when I had to."

"To the death?"

"Only when I had to."

"Well, this isn't one of those times. Third blood and there's no need for either of us to get hurt. Keep the blade light, just scratches, you understand, and we'll both have something to show for it. One fifth to the loser, right?"

A change but Dumarest wasn't deluded into thinking the man was genuine. He would kill or cripple so badly that death would be a mercy. The talk was to gain an added advantage, to pander to his warped nature. He would gain extra pleasure in the deception should it work.

"Knives!" An attendant came towards them, a pair of

37

blades in his hands. Ten-inches of naked steel, hilts of heavy brass, points like needles. But they were badly balanced, awkward to the hand.

"I'll use my own," said Dumarest.

"It's an inch shorter."

"So I'll give an advantage." He held out his hand towards Galbrio. "Let me see your knife."

"Why not?" The man handed it over. "Now let me check yours."

Both were looking for the same thing, the minute hole which would reveal a secret mechanism; a dart projector which could spit a missile coated with a numbing poison or a gas projector which would spray a noxious vapor into an opponent's eyes. Such devices gave one chance only but, correctly used, they would ensure victory.

Both knives were clean, and taking his, Dumarest led the way into the ring. A scatter of applause greeted him. It rose to a thunder as Galbrio appeared, bowing, smirking at the crowd.

"Kill him, Galbrio!" yelled a man. "Kill him!"

The fighter answered with a smile.

Dumarest did not smile. He stood, waiting, poised in the little circle, knife in hand and every muscle tense.

Now, as always, he was conscious of the fact that this could be his last fight. That here, in this ring, he could end both his search and his life.

Chapter FOUR

~~~~~~~~~~~~~~~~~~~~~~~~~~~~

The announcements were brief; the sound of a bell and it began. Above, the massed lights threw down a savage brilliance, their heat bringing sweat to dew the skin, thinning the film of oil which most fighters used to numb the pain of cuts and to prevent an opponent gaining a grip with his free hand. Beneath his naked feet Dumarest could feel the rough surface of the taut plastic covering the platform. Around him he could sense the impact of watching eyes.

The air stank of blood-lust and the feral anticipation of pain.

Dumarest ignored it as he did the watching eyes. Here, in this little circular universe, only one thing was of importance: the man who faced him and who intended to take his life—who would take it unless he was beaten first.

Dumarest thought of the young man he had seen carried from the ring after falling to Galbrio's blade. He had been lying on the table, screaming, one eye gone, his left arm useless, intestines oozing from a slashed stomach, his body traced with deep gashes showing the white points of severed tendons.

A moment, then even that memory was dissolved and all

became concentrated in the man facing him, his eyes, his feet and hands, the glimmer of his knife.

A glimmer which flashed into sparkles as he twisted the blade, using it as a mirror to send dazzling brilliance into Dumarest's eyes.

An old trick and one he had expected but he backed a little, blinking, obviously thrown off balance. Galbrio swallowed the bait and came in, dancing, crouched, his knife slashing to halt, to sweep back in a vicious reverse cut, to lance upwards in a cutting stab towards the stomach.

A blow which would have slit the abdomen had it landed, spilling guts and blood in a mess of pipes and vital fluids. One which, instead, clashed against Dumarest's protecting blade which then moved as he attacked in turn, the edge dipping, biting, dragging free with a shower of carmine rain.

"He's hit!" The crowd yelled as Galbrio backed, scowling, the gaping ruby mouth on his left bicep dripping blood.

A blow which had almost reached the bone and could have been sent against the corded throat had Dumarest wished. But it was not his intention to kill the man.

He moved as Galbrio turned, careful of the blood now dappling the floor, knowing that a careless step could turn victory into defeat. Always, in any fight, there was the danger of the unknown. Blood, oil, grease, a trifling misjudgment and balance could be lost and the fight with it.

Again the blades met, ringing, parting to meet again in a flurry of steel. A second wound joined the first, across the torso this time, as deep as those Galbrio had given earlier. A third, and he backed, eyes wide, fear distorting his scarred face.

"Fast," he said. "God, you're fast! I quit. I don't stand a chance. Here."

He lifted his knife as if to throw it down, to send the point into the platform in the signal of surrender. A move never completed for, as his arm moved downwards, it changed direction, developed power, sent the naked steel spinning through the air towards Dumarest. A gambler's trick, should it fail the man would be left unarmed and defenseless, but at such close quarters, against a man who had lowered his guard, such a move would work more often than not.

Dumarest moved, his own knife lifting, steel ringing as he slammed his own blade against the hurtling weapon. It thrummed through the air and landed to quiver in the floor at Galbrio's feet.

"Pick it up," said Dumarest.

"I've quit!"

"You've tried one trick too many. Pick it up or take what's coming with empty hands."

He wasn't making an empty threat and the man knew it. For a moment he stared into Dumarest's eyes then, snarling, stooped, snatched free the knife and with the frenzied courage of a man who has nothing to lose, hurled himself forward.

And died as Dumarest slammed his knife upwards into the heart.

In the dressing room Benny said, "Why? What made you do it?"

"Money."

"Just that?" He frowned, thought for a moment, then shrugged. "I can't understand fighters. Who knows what goes on inside the head of a man who risks his life for a living? But I'll tell you this. You want money I'll arrange a bout any time you choose. I've never seen anyone move so fast. Galbrio should have got you. It was a dirty trick and he deserved all you gave him but he should have got you. So, friend, any time you want a bout let me know."

"I will."

"Just remember that. Anything I can do for you?"

"Yes," said Dumarest. "Just make sure I'm not followed."

He was three times richer than when he had entered the place, still not enough to pay what Hilda Benson had asked but maybe enough to meet the new requirements as set by her friend. And, on this world as on any other, a man with money was a target for trouble. Twice he halted, listening, moving on only when satisfied no one was following. Three times he changed direction, doubling back on himself and ending, finally, far to one side of the field.

It was busy, a file of men working like ants as they unloaded a freighter, piling bales and crates on wheeled trolleys which were dragged away. All looked alike, thin, stooped, gaunt, dressed in a collection of rags. It was close to dawn and they shivered in the chill air despite the heat induced by their efforts. An overseer stood to one side, checking something on a board.

"Right, Emmanuel. Take a score of workers and haul this stuff to warehouse eighteen. Andre, you take as many and shift all the Qualan stock to warehouse nine. Don't forget to check at the gate."

"Right." Two men dressed in warm clothing stepped away, halting as the overseer called after them.

"You'd better hire a couple of guards each from the gate."

"What for?" Andre, short, stocky, spat his disgust. "I can handle these creeps."

"Sure you can, did I say different? Think of it as insurance. If one falls down and breaks his neck they can take care of it. Right?"

"As you say, boss. Just as you say."

Dumarest watched as the little columns moved towards the gate. Cheap labor from the pool and regarded as little better than dirt. To the guards they would be faceless creatures, to the overseers the same. They would live and die and the only difference between one and another was how long they would take to finally give up.

It began to rain again as he moved around the field and a thin wind rose to drive the stinging drops into his eyes as he reentered the town. The place seemed deserted, not even a guard to be seen, and he looked in vain for a cab. The day broke as he reached the plaza and he halted at a small restaurant in a back street which, for some reason, had opened early. The coffee was poor but hot and welcome and, from the conversation of others, he gathered that the place was open early to serve the porters in the nearby market.

When he left the streets were coming to life—Harald was an early-rising world.

Armand Ramhed, it seemed, wasn't.

Dumarest paused in the tiny hall and closed the door behind him. The house was dark and held an eerie stillness. There should have been sound of some kind, a snore, a movement, the echo of heavy breathing at least. Instead there was nothing.

Cautiously he moved towards the kitchen, half-expecting to find Armand lying across the table, too drunk to stand. The place was deserted. The rear rooms the same. Gently Dumarest pushed open the door of the study.

"Armand?" He stepped into the room when there was no answer. "Armand. Wake up, damn you. Wake up!"

He couldn't.

Armand Ramhed was dead.

He lay on the table at which he worked, his head on the scanner, fitful gleams of colored brilliance painting his face as they had before. But now there was nothing of the clown about the thin temples and sunken cheeks. There was only the pathetic shell of what had once been a man who had died while engrossed in his hobby. A good way to go, perhaps, but Dumarest wished that he had waited. Or perhaps the man had finished what he'd set out to do?

Gently Dumarest lifted the frail shape and placed it in a chair. Switching on the main lights he looked around the room. The table held a litter of papers, notes, figures, equations. Sheets held spectrographic schematics each traced with a heavy pattern of lines. Thick tomes were opened at pages listing the Fraunhofer identity of spectral elements. The scanner, obviously, held his strip of film.

Dumarest opened it and removed the spectrogram. Holding it he again examined the table. Armand had been working until the last, he would have made notes or, at least, finalized some of his data. If he had, where would they be?

Dumarest frowned, conscious that something was wrong. An item missing, one present which shouldn't be, something set different to what he remembered. The glass? Had the glass rested on the wad of papers when he'd left? Armand had waved farewell, too engrossed to turn, grunting as Dumarest had warned him he might be late. What had he said?

Something about wine?

Memory stirred and came to life. Bring back some wine, Earl? Or had it been, Help yourself to wine? Wine? The glass, perhaps?

Lifting it Dumarest sniffed. It was empty but he could smell the sickly residue clinging to the glass. It told him nothing. But would Armand have been content with a single glass of wine?

In the kitchen Dumarest dropped to his knees and examined the floor, not even sure of what he was looking for but, conscious only of a nagging unease. The instinct which warned his that something was wrong. He found it in the vat of fermenting liquid.

The level, as he remembered, had been high. A fresh brew, Armand had told him, one which he'd hoped to nurture but which he had been driven to use. Now the level was much lower than it had been. Two bottles at least had been removed, perhaps three.

If Armand had drunk them he must have done it out here. The bottles were as he remembered, dusty, empty, grimed. The man must have sat and dipped and drank and dipped again and drank until he had fallen into a stupor where he sat.

And, drunk, how could he have returned to the study and sat and concentrated on his work?

He rested where Dumarest had placed him, his eyes open, glazed, his features waxen in the cold light. One hand hung limply, the fingers touching the dusty floor, the other was clenched and pressed tightly against his side. Dumarest eased open the fingers and stared at what lay in the palm. A button traced with a design in amber on black. A stylized dragon, he thought, or some mathematical symbol used for ornamentation. Armand's button? The man's clothes were thin and of poor quality, the buttons made of some plastic material, plain and functional. And none were missing.

Reaching out Dumarest closed the staring eyes then froze, his hand touching the waxen cheeks, his eyes narrowing as they spotted the trace of bruises, a thin smear of blood.

It rested beneath the lobe of the ear, a touch previously hidden by the kaleidoscope of color thrown by the scanner. The light was white, now, a cold glare from the unshaded bulb and in it the smear showed plain. Turning the head Dumarest lifted the ear and found the answer lying beneath.

A small wound, almost lost, sealed by the natural contraction of the skin and muscle behind the ear. One made by something long and thin, a heavy bodkin or a knitting needle, either would have done. A pointed sliver of metal which had been thrust into the softness behind the ear until the point had lacerated the brain. Death would have been instantaneous.

As assassins's trick—the wound, self-sealing, prevented a tell-tale show of blood. At a casual glance the victim would appear to be lost in thought and, had the eyes been closed, asleep. But why had they been left open? Why the betraying smear?

Carelessness induced by haste. The work of an amateur. The eyes could have been overlooked, the smear left when the killing instrument had been withdrawn.

Murder—but why?

What reason to kill an old man? His poverty was obvious and even if a thief had been at work there was no sign of any search. Someone had gained admittance to the house, found Armand lying drunk, had killed him and carefully placed him in his chair in the study. Obviously the drunken stupor had not been total. The bruises showed signs of a struggle, the button proof that the assassin's intent had been recognized even if too late.

But, again, why?

Why kill a harmless old man?

Dumarest lifted a hand to his throat already feeling the weight of a collar. Instinct had saved him. Finding Armand dead he should have called the guards. They would have held him for questioning, an examination would show the manner of death, automatically he would have been suspect.

And, on Harald, once a man wore a collar there could be no escape.

Trapped, helpless to run, he would have no choice but to wait.

Dumarest looked at the button in his hand. The symbol was meaningless but, to him, it bore a familiar stamp. Not the design itself but the stealth and guile it represented. Amber on black but it might well have been a more familiar design traced on scarlet. The seal of the Cyclan.

They must be very close.

Dumarest turned to the table, again searching, papers flying as he burrowed into the litter. If Armand had relaxed enough to yield to the lure of wine then he must have finished his task. Somewhere, in the mess, must be the final pattern of lines or a series of figures or a compacted code of some kind which other experts would recognize. He froze as voices came from outside.

"A scream, officer, I swear it. I thought nothing of it at the time but it's been worrying me. The old man could have had an accident. I tried the door but it's locked."

"And he had a visitor, you say?"

"Yes." The voice hesitated then, firmly, said, "A tough-looking character. From the field by the look of him. That's what got me to worrying. If he thought the old man had money hidden away—well, I thought I'd report it."

The jaws of the trap snapping fast. Obviously there had been a watcher, the assassin himself, perhaps. When Dumarest had shown no sign of calling the guards he had been forced to act.

Dumarest ran from the study into the bedroom. From a wardrobe he pulled cloaks, blankets, assorted clothing. All were old, frayed, thin with age. They ripped easily between his hands.

As a pounding came from the front door he stooped, wrapped swathes of material around his boots, more around his thighs, rough wadding which he held with knotted strands. A stained blouse over his tunic and a faded cloak over that and he was done. The rest of the disguise must lie in his stance and movements.

The front door shook beneath the impact of a boot. The voice of the watcher rose above the hammering.

"I'd better go around the back, officer. If I see him I'll call out."

Another mistake, the man should have had others watching, but it was one to Dumarest's advantage. He reached the back door, opened it, threw it wide then stepped back as footsteps pounded towards him. Outside the rain had increased to a steady downpour, the air misted with flying droplets, the wind spattering a moist hail. The figure which suddenly appeared was young, the hair roached and sparkling with wetness, the face smooth and innocent. He wore a dull green jacket with a high, flared collar and ornamented lapels. The buttons were discs of ebon traced with an amber design. One was missing, a loop of thread showing from where it had been torn.

A man dressed for a party who had been standing unprotected in the rain. A man who was not what he seemed.

His face changed as he saw the open door and he ran towards it, mouth opened to shout, a shout which died unborn as Dumarest lunged towards him. They met in the portal, the assassin grabbing at something beneath his jacket, Dumarest already in action. His right hand rose up and forward, the palm turned outwards, the fingers curved backwards. The heel of his hand skidded up over the mouth striking the nostrils with the full force of his arm, back and shoulder.

A blow which crushed cartilage, smashed delicate bone, drove the splinters upwards through the space between the eyes, shards which thrust like daggers through the thin point of the skull and into the brain.

An old hat had been among Armand Ramhed's effects. Dumarest pulled it over his face as the assassin fell, jumping over the body which had slumped in the doorway and walking without hesitation across the untidy garden. An alley lay beyond a fence, deserted aside from a scavenger.

The man didn't bother to look up from the heap of garbage he was examining for items of worth. Ramhed had been poor, the area reflected his poverty, it was enough for a man to take care of himself. And it was raining with a wind which drove stinging droplets into the eyes.

Head down, shoulders stooped, trudging like a man on the edge of exhaustion, Dumarest headed into the city.

Chapter FIVE

~~~~~~

As a boy Cyber Broge had been taught that to be impatient was to be unwise; a lesson emphasized with the coldly efficient skill of the Cyclan long before he was permitted to wear the scarlet robe which now clothed his sparse figure. The lesson, like all the others which had been taught, like all the things which had been done to make him what he now was, had served its intent. But, even so, he wished that the work in which he was now involved could be less than it was.

A wish which died as soon as it was formed; to long for the unattainable was an insult to intelligence and to chafe against necessity a mental irritation.

"Cyber Broge?" The man before him was a merchant dealing in grain, furs, oils and rare perfumes. A native of Harald and a wealthy representative of his class. He had paid for the interview and intended to make the most of it.

"Well?"

"Should I concentrate on accumulating grain or would it be better to sell what I have and invest the money in furs?" He fumbled with some papers, a little uneasy beneath the cyber's unwavering stare. "Or should I increase my stock of perfumes?"

"They come from where?"

"Vandalia. Essences of emphrige, olten and plenia."

"The primary of Vandalia has shown increased turbulence of the photosphere and this will, inevitably, disturb the normal tranquility of local space. There could be an emission of unusual radiation which could affect the plants producing the oils you mention. The probability of that happening is seventy-three per cent."

"High?"

"As stated." The cyber's voice was an even modulation devoid of irritant factors. "The fashionable preference for the wearing of furs will fade as a result of a singer now achieving fame who has stated her dislike of wearing the skins of slaughtered beasts."

"Is that a fact?"

"It is a probability of ninety-two percent."

"High?"

"As stated."

"Almost a certainty?" The merchant hesitated, wanting to press then, remembering the fee he had paid, went ahead. "It is certain the market for fashion-furs will fall?"

"Nothing is certain," said the cyber evenly. "My prediction is based on an assessment of known data and the probability is as stated."

"Then you advise me to—"

"I do not advise." The tones remained as even as before but, even so, the rebuke was plain. "I do not guide. As a servant of the Cyclan I merely inform you of the logical development of events. What action you choose to take is up to you." Reaching out a hand he touched a bell and, as an acolyte appeared, gestured towards the door.

The interview was over and another followed at once, this time a man who represented a consortium manufacturing small electronic components who was eager to know market trends on the world which took their exports. He was followed by a woman interested in discovering which of three suitors would be the best match for her only daughter. Then two others also interested in business, a matron seeking investment-advice, an old man worried about his health.

He was followed by a politician.

Guy Herylin was smooth, shrewd, ambitious. An election was to be held in a northern sector and he wanted to win it. He also wanted to know what path he should take to gain the greatest advantage. Money would help—but who to bribe?

The cyber heard him out, his face expressionless, his mind working as he assessed the facts presented to him, extrapolated from them, gauged the man and set him against what he knew of his opponents. They too were ambitious but a little less ruthless. Pressure could be applied against them, their influence would wane, Herylin would take over and, the higher he climbed, the more he would come to rely on the services of the Cyclan.

An old, old pattern and one which every cyber helped to weave. Men and women of influence, coming for help and guidance, listening to the predictions and being subtly maneuvered by them. A blight discovered in a distant region which would pass to the estates of a highly placed politician which would, in turn, present a financial disaster. One which could be aggravated by a clever buying of stock in advance, of selling it high, of ruining an opponent by an apparent use of coincidental good fortune.

A system which had proved its worth on a scatter of worlds throughout the galaxy. Plants which were ruled in fact if not in name by the servants of the organization to which Broge belonged. Scarlet-robed cybers, always ready to make their predictions, to take a handful of facts and from them to extrapolate the most logical sequence of events. Almost, to those who used them, it seemed they could predict the future and actions, based on those predictions, made them actualities.

Now, to Guy Herylin, he said, "The representative of your region has suffered from a heart condition within the past two weeks. He is addicted to hunting and, if he should continue his sport the possibility is that he will suffer another attack shortly after commencing the chase. Should that happen the prediction of you being elected to take his place is eighty-four per cent." Pausing he added, "Assuming the attack is fatal, naturally."

"And if it isn't?"

"There are too many variables at this time for a firm prediction. He could linger for months and his party take steps to lift another of their choosing to his place."

"So, at the present time, the key to my advancement lies in the possibility of my opponent having a second attack? A fatal one?"

"Exactly."

"I see." Herylin rose from where he had been sitting. "You couldn't advise how such a thing could be accomplished, I suppose?"

"We of the Cyclan do not advise. We—"

"Do not take sides." Herylin was curt in his interruption. "I know. You don't have to spell it out for me. You are neutral observers and only give predictions of varying orders of probability. Well, thanks anyway."

He had been rude and would later have time to realize how foolish he had been. The services of the Cyclan were not cheap and not to be had on demand. After he had managed to dispose of his opponent, Herylin would become a tried and tested weapon to be used in the domination of his world.

The man would have no choice. Ringed as he would be by others as ambitious as himself Guy Herylin had to rely on the predictions of a cyber. What course would this particular piece of legislation follow? What would be the outcome of such and such introduction to the laws? How best to raise taxation? How else to discover weaknesses and trends? To be apparently in advance of public opinion? To always seem to be leading while others followed, always too late with too little?

Slowly he would be broken, slowly bent to the will of his masters as an animal to the desires of its owner. Then he would learn that it did not pay to be rude to any cyber. That it could be fatal to defy the power of the Cyclan.

Broge felt the glow of mental satisfaction.

He was young, sent to this small and isolated world to help the Great Design, a cog yet to prove himself. But already the work had begun and soon he could dispense with the minor irritations; the women who sought advice despite his denial of giving it, those who had small problems of

51

only personal importance, the interviews with those who only wanted to gain wealth.

"Master!" The acolyte was standing before him. "The anteroom is empty. Only Captain Kregor waits."

The police chief of the city and the cyber could guess what his report would be. Again he felt the glow of mental satisfaction and realized, even as he felt it, that he had lacked the right to earn it. Circumstances and the shrewd predictions of others had brought it about. He merely happened to be at the right place at the right time, and yet, small though his part had been, it set the seal on the work of others and would not be forgotten.

"Send him in."

Kregor had been kept waiting for an hour and was far from pleased. He strode towards the desk, a thick-set, burly man with a shock of reddish hair and a face seamed and creased with weather and time. His uniform, the cyber noted, was rumpled and his boots stained by water and dirt. True it had been raining again but was the man so careless as to personal appearances?

In return the captain stared his dislike at the figure robed in scarlet.

Kregor didn't like the cyber. He didn't like any of the breed. Men should look like men, not gaunt, skeletal shapes with faces like skulls, shaven, the eyes alone burning with life. A man should enjoy his food and wine and the weaknesses of the flesh; those who could feel no pain or pleasure, who used food as fuel and could neither hate nor fear were something other than human. Robots, living machines, creatures who had been operated on at puberty and who could feel nothing but the pleasure of mental achievement.

Slaves to the organization the seal of which was emblazoned on the creast of the scarlet robe.

Cybers!

Yet he had no choice but to cooperate and, if he was wise, to be polite.

"Captain?" Broge was waiting. "You have something to report?"

"Yes."

"The man Dumarest is safe in custody?" The cyber rose,

guessing the answer from the captain's expression. "He isn't? What happened?"

"Nothing happened."

"Don't be too precise with me, Captain. Not if you value your rank and employment." The tones were as evenly modulated as always but there was no mistaking the implication. Not a threat, the Cyclan never threatened, simply a statement of the obvious. A prediction with an order of probability verging on certainty. "All that was needed was to take the man into custody and hold him. Why was that not done?"

"No reason was given."

"The request, surely, was enough?"

"On any other world, perhaps." Kregor squared his shoulders; once he had killed a wild beast with his bare hands while out hunting, why should he fear a machine clad in scarlet? "A general awareness was maintained as a matter of courtesy and you were notified when he landed."

"And?"

"Nothing. We knew of the man, he couldn't leave without our knowledge and, if he had tried to leave, he would have been held. Again," he added, stiffly, "as a matter of courtesy."

A barrier and one which the cyber had expected. The influence of the Cyclan was small as yet on this world, yet strong enough to ensure that Dumarest, once held, would be quietly handed over without fuss or trial. The agent he had used should have seen to it that the man had been held. What had gone wrong?

He listened as the captain told him, his face remaining impassive, his thoughts a flickering, darting turmoil. The agent had failed, that was obvious, and had died as a result of his inadequacy. But where was Dumarest now?

Kregor shrugged as he put the question. "I don't know as yet."

"But you've been looking? A murderer, surely, can't be allowed to escape."

"Did I say he was a murderer?"

"A man was dead, you say."

"True, but we lack proof that Dumarest intended to kill him. It could have been an accident. The man was armed

53

and may have threatened Dumarest who struck out in self-defence. It was a most unusual blow. It—"

"Take me to see him," ordered the cyber. "I want to see them both."

It was cold in the mortuary but Broge didn't feel the chill. He stood, impassively waiting, the cowl lifted to frame his gaunt features as an attendant slid the long, narrow table from the wall. The agent was difficult to recognize with his destroyed face.

"Bram Jolpen," said Kregor. "His father owns a mill to the south. Rich, spoiled, a bit of a playboy. He'd taken a young girl home—or so he told an officer, when he heard a scream. It worried him—or so he claimed, and he went to find someone to investigate."

"You seem doubtful that he was telling the truth."

"It seems odd. A young man in a poor area who stood in the rain for no apparent reason. We haven't been able to find the girl. We can't find anyone who drove him to the spot. He was armed."

"So?"

"If armed then why wait to find an officer if he was so concerned? When he heard the scream he could have gone to investigate. At least he could have banged on the door."

Broge said, "But you are certain Dumarest killed him."

"No." Kregor was emphatic. "I'm not certain at all. There were no witnesses and think of that blow! Well, look at it. He could have aimed a punch at the jaw and Jolpen stepped back so that it caught his nose. An accident."

"Then why not stay?"

"He could have been afraid. Maybe he thought there were others after him like Jolpen. How do I know why he ran?" Kregor scowled as he looked at the dead man. "An accident," he rumbled. "We'd never be able to convict on evidence like that."

It had been no accident and the cyber knew it. The angle of the blow for one thing and the tremendous force with which it had been delivered. If it came to it medical testimony could be called in to question the captain's assumption of accident, but that shouldn't be necessary.

"And the other man?"

"Armand Ramhed?" Kregor gestured at the attendant.

Jolpen had done his work too well.

Lying on the slab the old man looked at peace. They had folded his hands and combed his hair and he seemed more asleep than dead.

"We found him sitting in a chair," explained Kregor. "My guess it that he had just felt tired, sat for a moment then fell asleep. He just didn't wake up."

"The other man reported he heard a scream."

"So?"

"Dumarest was staying with the old man. He could have tortured him."

"Why? Money?" Kregor frowned and shook his head. "The man had nothing and any fool would have known it. Why torture an old man for nothing?"

"Need a criminal have logical explanations for what he does?" The cyber glanced at the attendant. "What did the autopsy show?"

Glancing at the captain the man said, "There hasn't been one."

"Don't you know how he died?"

"Natural causes, I guess." The man was defiant. "And he wasn't tortured—there isn't a mark on him."

"But the scream—"

"We have only Jolpen's word for that," said the captain. He sounded impatient. "There's no point in making work, Cyber Broge. I've my men out looking for Dumarest and when we find him he will tell us what really happened."

"If you find him."

"We will." The captain was brusk. "I've men at all points. He might even give himself up once he's had time to think it over. Why not? An unlucky blow struck in fear—who could blame him?"

It was pointless to argue and could even be awkward. If he mentioned how the old man had been killed then Kregor would be curious as to how he knew. Also once an association had been formed between his knowledge and the assassin, details best left hidden might be exposed.

But Dumarest had to be found.

Broge stood thinking, assembling facts, assessing known data. A man on the run, a stranger in the city, where would he go to hide?

He said, "Captain, was anything taken from the house?"

"Not as far as we know."

"Nothing disturbed?"

"Papers on the desk. And some clothing. It was scattered before a wardrobe; old stuff not worth a beggar's notice. As I told you the old man was poor."

"But—"

"What now?" With an effort Kregor mastered his irritation. He was tired and cold and was more worried than he cared to admit. The failure to find Dumarest was evidence of inefficiency, a fact the dead youth's father would make the most of at the enquiry. Bram Jolpen had been a wastrel, but his family would be thirsting for revenge and would be vicious if denied it. He must give them no grounds for complaint and it was no time to make powerful enemies. He had gone too far and knew it. "My apologies, Cyber Broge, I did not mean to be discourteous. But I assure you that I have done, and am doing, all I can to find the missing man. It is only a matter of time."

"What if he should manage to gain passage on a ship?"

"He can't. The field is secured. Only one vessel has left since the incident and that was two hours after the dead were found. He couldn't have obtained passage on the *Accaus*. We'll get him, Cyber Broge. I promise you." He looked at the old man lying on his slab. "Is there anything else I can do for you?"

"Thank you, no, Captain. We both have other matters claiming our attention."

From the mortuary Broge returned directly to his quarters. A small room opened from his office, bleak, containing little more than a narrow couch. A cyber needed little else. He wasted no energy carrying a load of useless, waterlogged tissue and had no time for emotionally stimulating art work. Intellectually he could appreciate the beauty of functional design but, that a thing served its purpose, was all that was required. A bed did not have to be too wide, too soft, too ornate. That it provided support and the room in which it rested privacy, was all a cyber could demand.

"Master!" His acolyte bowed as he was summoned. "Has the man been found?"

"No."

"Your orders?"

"Check with the men watching Hilda Benson. Have them search her home. It is barely possible she is aiding him."

"Dumarest? But, master, she informed us where he was to be found."

"Which means nothing. Women are difficult to predict with any high degree of accuracy. The death of her old friend could have created a state of aberration."

"It will be done, master. And?"

"Total seal."

Broge touched the heavy band locked around his left wrist as, bowing, the acolyte left the small room and closed the door. Protection enough against invasion, but the mechanism incorporated into the band gave more. A flood of invisible energy streamed from it creating a field which provided a barrier against any prying electronic eye or ear.

Lying supine on the couch Broge closed his eyes and concentrated on the Samatachazi formulae. The initial state was difficult to achieve and he forced himself to relax, remembering his instructions, the guides he had been given during early training. Later, he knew, the act would become second-nature and, always, it was a mistake to let urgency intrude.

There was no need for haste . . . no need . . . no need . . .

Gradually he lost sensory perception; the senses of touch, of hearing, of smell, of taste. Had he opened his eyes he would have been blind. Reality ceased to exist as the part of an external universe and his brain, locked within the boney protection of his skull, ceased to be irritated by external stimuli. It turned in on itself, became a world of its own, a new sphere of existence concerned only with reason and untrammeled intellect. A state of nirvana in which nothing existed or could exist but the egotistical self. And then, like tiny fires burning on a nighted horizon, the grafted Homochon elements became active.

Rapport was established.

Broge became something more than human.

His brain expanded, his awareness swelling like a collossal balloon to encompass all of time and creation. Sheets and planes of scintillant brilliance were all around and he could see them all in perfect, over-all vision. Each cyber, he knew, had a different experience and none could reduce to words the ecstasy of the unfolding. For him it was as if he moved bodiless through showers of broken rainbows; splinters of unsuspected color woven as if in a fantastic tapestry of unimaginable complexity, a three-dimensional web of translucent hues, intangible yet each strand containing a fragment of the space-time continuum in a series of ever-multiplying, ever-changing relationships.

An incredible maze of which he was an integral part, immersed in the radiance so that it became an extension of his being and he became a manifestation of its complexity, the part merging with and transmuted into the whole.

Like a shimmer of brilliant rain, shards and sparkles of scintillant hue, curtains of gossamer laced and riven with an infinity of strands the fabric of intermeshed rainbows turned and curved and led to a common center at the heart of which lay the headquarters of the Cyclan.

It blazed with the cold, clear light of pure intelligence. The complex which dominated the entire organization, correlating it, synchronizing effort, plotting the devious moves and counter moves strung over a multitude of worlds. The Central Intelligence which, even as he grew aware of it, made contact: merging, touching, assimilating his knowledge and making it its own. Mental communication of incredible swiftness.

"*Dumarest on Harald?*"

Affirmation.

"*But not in your custody. Explain the failure.*"

Reasons.

"*The use of an inefficient agent is a fault. You are to be blamed for that. The probability that Dumarest managed to escape on the* Accaus *is low. The time element was against this. Another fault.*"

Protestation.

"*Agreed. The distance could have been covered by an agile man in the time specified and a heavy bribe could have gained both entrance to the field and a passage, yet the probability is a mere eight per cent. Even so steps will be taken. Men will be waiting at the world of destination. Future intent?*"

Explanation.

"*Accepted. The probability of Dumarest still being within the city is high. He must be captured at all costs. All precautions must be taken to ensure his protection. Under no circumstances must he be killed. Give this matter your personal attention. Dumarest must be taken. Failure will not be tolerated.*"

Understanding.

"*Find and capture Dumarest and immediate preference will be yours. Fail and you know the penalty. Do not fail!*"

The rest was euphoria.

Always, after rapport, there was a period during which the grafted Homochon elements sank again into quiescence and the physical machinery of the body began to realign itself with the dictates of the brain and, during that time, the mind was assailed by a storm of ungoverned impressions.

Broge drifted in a lightless void, detached, a pure brain in an environment in which only the cold light of reason could prevail. He experienced a host of exotic stimuli, memories of places he had never seen, knowledge he had not gained, knew situations alien to his frames of reference—all the over-spill from other minds, fragments, the discard of a conglomerate of assembled intelligences. The waste, in a sense, of the tremendous cybernetic complex which was the hidden power of the Cyclan.

One day he would become a part of it. His body would age and grow rebellious, senses would dull and reactions slow but his mind would remain the keen instrument training and use had made it. Then he would be summoned, taken on the final journey to a secret place where his brain would be removed from his skull, placed in a vat of nutrients, connected in series to the other brains previously assembled. A countless host of intelligences which, working in harmony, formed the Central Intelligence.

There he would remain for eternity, maintained, supported, working to the common end, the prime directive of the Cyclan. All the problems of the universe to be solved, all Mankind to be united into an efficient whole, all waste eliminated, harmony to be achieved beneath the dictates of the Cyclan. The Great Design of which he was a living part.

Chapter SIX

~~~~~~~~~~~~~~~~~~~~~~~~~~~~

Dumarest woke feeling the touch of fingers, questing, probing like a predatory spider. He lay still, eyes slitted as they peered into darkness. He could hear the soft breathing of someone close and then, as gentle as a landing butterfly, the chill impact of something like ice at his throat.

Not ice and not a butterfly but a jagged sliver of glass held by the man who searched him, resting, poised ready to rip into his flesh, to slash the great arteries and release his life in a fountain of blood should he move.

Lowtown was not a gentle place.

He could smell the stench of it around him; the stink of unwashed flesh pressed too close, bodies huddled together for the sake of warmth, vapors rising from damp clothing. The whole compounded with the odors of sickness and running sores, of disease, of grime and rancid oil, of scraps of mouldering food.

Of the poverty which ruled here in this place on this world.

The searching hand grew more bold, the fingers tugging at the fastening of the cloak, slipping inside to fumble at the blouse, the wadded belt beneath. Dumarest felt the touch of breath on his cheek, air carrying a fetid odor which caught at his nostrils. The sharp fragment resting on his throat lifted a little as the man, growing careless, concentrated on the bulk his fingers had found.

A little more and it would be time to act yet to wait too long would be to betray too much. Dumarest gently drew in his breath, tensed his muscles and, with a blur of movement, had rolled away from the threatening shard, had turned, caught the searching hand, squeezing it as the man reared back like a startled beast.

"You—"

The glass had driven its point into the dirt. The glass shattered as Dumarest slammed the heel of his free hand against it, lifting the fingers to snatch at the other wrist. Trapped, body arched back from the hands which held it fast, the man glared his hate and fear.

"My hand! My wrist! Don't!"

"You were robbing me!"

"No! I—." The man swallowed, his adam's apple bobbing in his scrawny throat, his face pale in the dim light cast by the external lights. "I thought you were a friend."

"Liar!" Dumarest closed his hands a little. "Thief!"

"No!" The man sweated with pain. "For God's sake, kill me if you want but don't break my bones!"

He was starving, desperate, driven to act the wolf. It would be charity to give him money for food to thrust into his empty belly but to do that would be to commit suicide. Even if he didn't talk others would notice and, like vicious wasps, they would be eager for their share of what was going. And the man himself would never be satisfied. It was better policy to kill him—a thief had no right to expect mercy.

"Do it," said the man. He had the courage of a cornered rat. "If you're going to kill me make it fast and clean but, before you strike ask yourself if you're in any position to judge. Haven't you ever turned thief when you had no other choice?"

Thief and killer; money stolen from purses when he'd been a boy, other things when, older, he'd grown delirious with hunger. Men killed for the sake of gain. Butchered in the arena for the enjoyment of a crowd. Had Galbrio deserved to die? Had any of the others who had wagered themselves against his skill and lost?

And there had been others—the law of life was simple.

Survive!

Live no matter what the cost for, without life, there is nothing. Live!

Kill or be killed!

"Mister?"

"Go to hell!" Dumarest pushed the man away so that he fell to sprawl in the mud. "Come near me again and I'll break your neck!"

"You were a fool," said the huddled shape at his side when he settled down again beneath the scrap of fabric which formed the roof of a crude shelter. "You should have killed him. His boots would have been worth a bowl of soup, his clothes another." The man began to cough, liquid gurglings rising from fluid-filled lungs. "The bastard! I've no time for thieves."

"That makes two of us."

"Yet you let him go. That shows you're new here. Come in on the last ship?" He coughed again as Dumarest grunted. "I've been here most of a year now. Arrived after travelling Low. I had money, enough for another passage once I'd got my fat back, but they wouldn't let me leave the field. A High passage or nothing—you know the system. Well, I wasn't all that worried, a few days and there'd be another ship, a month, say, and I'd get fit for the journey. Then some bastard stole my money."

He fell silent, thinking, remembering the awful bleakness of the discovery. The regret at not having spent the cash while he'd had the chance. Of buying himself some small luxuries, some decent clothes, enjoying the pleasures of a women, maybe.

"I never found who stole it," he continued after another fit of coughing. "But it was summer and the harvest was due and workers were needed. Given time, I figured, I could build another stake. And the rest would do me good." His laugh was ugly. "Rest! They worked the tail off me for little more than the price of a day's food. Out before dawn and back after dark. We lived in tents way out past the city. There were overseers with whips and, if you slacked, they docked your pay." He added, dully, "I guess you know the rest."

A familiar pattern. Cheap labor kept that way by the lack of choice. A strong man would last especially in summer and autumn, then would come winter and the wastage of precious tissue, the sapping of strength, energy lost merely to keep warm. By spring only the strongest would be able to work. The rest would lie, faces becoming little more than eyes, bodies shrunken to less than the weight of a child. Disease would be kind then, robbing life with merciful swiftness.

Rising, Dumarest stepped from the shelter and looked around. It was close to dawn, the sky beginning to pale, the only light coming from the standards ringing the field and from where a fire threw a patch of warmth and brilliance to one side. Around and above stretched a cage of thick wire mesh, a hemisphere pierced by a single opening which led to the field. It was barred now but an hour after dawn the barrier would be opened and vendors coming from the city would offer scraps of food to any who could pay.

Those who couldn't could only beg, thrusting fingers and hands through the mesh to those who came strolling past during the afternoon and evening. Sightseers out to look at the animals. Those who brought food with them were kind.

It wasn't their fault Lowtown existed. No one had forced these within the cage to come to their world. They had no duty to support the uninvited guests. Why should they deny themselves so that others, who had done nothing to earn the largess, should gain?

So let them work if they could or leave if they had the money or die if they couldn't.

No one in the whole wide galaxy had the right to charity. Only the strong deserved to survive.

A man sat at the edge of the fire playing a solitary game with a stained decks of cards. The warm glow shone on a hard face set with cold, deep-set eyes and a thin-lipped mouth. The chin was cleft. The hands were broad, the fingers spatulate, the nails blunt but neatly rounded.

He turned a card then looked up as Dumarest approached. "Sit," he invited. "Care for a game?"

"No."

"Anything you want." He turned a card and set it on another. "Starsmash, spectrum, high, low, man-in-between. Poker, khano, hunt-the-lady. Name the game and it's yours. You gamble?"

Dumarest said, dryly, "At times."

"But not now. Well, it was worth trying." The man picked up the cards, shuffled them, began to set them out for a game of solitaire. "Just arrived?"

"Yes."

"Then you must know the score. Sometimes it pays to string along. Sometimes it's suicide not to." He dropped the knave of swords on the lady of diamonds. "It took me a while to learn. Here it's dog eat dog, but I guess you know that. Have you money?"

Dumarest said, 'The ten of swords on the knave of hearts."

"So you're cautious, that's good. And I'd guess you know how to take care of yourself. Here there are only two kinds of people: sheep and wolves." He turned another card and set it into place. "I don't take you for a sheep."

"So?"

"There are ways to get along. Given time you'll find them and, if you were greedy, you'd want to take over. That would be a mistake." A card dropped from his fingers. "A man can get away from here if he puts his mind to it. It takes time but it can be done. I guess you know how."

A system as old as time. A strong and ruthless man taking over, arranging to hire out men and taking a cut from employers to avoid trouble, taking another from those they permitted to work. Small sums but they would accumulate. In time they would grow into the price of a passage—but Dumarest had no time.

He said, flatly, "I'm not ambitious."

"But you want to get away, right?" The man lifted his head, firelight gleaming from his eyes. In a shelter to one side, a man cried out in his sleep, falling silent with a fretful muttering. "To do that you've got to get out on the field. I can arrange it. Men will be wanted to load the ships. You'll have a chance to talk to the handlers and maybe pick up something. You know how it is, a bale or crate can split open by accident and only a fool would waste an opportunity." He riffled his cards. "I take a fifth of all you get."

Three ships waited on the field. "The *Ergun* was carrying a cargo of grain to a mining world and the handler smiled as Dumarest straightened after dumping the last sack into the hold.

"It wouldn't work," he said, quietly.

"What?"

"We fill the hold with prophane-X ten minutes after take-off. It's to kill any bugs but it'll take care of a man just as well. I mention it in case you know of anyone hoping to stowaway. He could do it—hell, who can check every sack, but he'd never make it alive."

"How about buying a passage?"

"Low?" The handler shook his head. "We've no caskets. It isn't worth keeping them on the run we do. Load up here, go to Zwen, move on to Cresh then back to here. Short trips."

Dumarest was blunt. "How much to let me ride? I'll pay what I can now, and give you a note so as you can collect from my earnings on Zwen. They take contract-workers, don't they? Well, it'll be just like money in the bank."

The handler thought about it, frowning. It was a mistake to trust the stranded, they would do anything, promise anything to get away. But this one seemed different. If he had the money and would be willing to pledge himself it was a good opportunity.

"I'll have to check."

"Must you?"

"The captain has to know." The handler was regretful. "With the hold sealed we ride close and there's no way to keep you out of sight. But don't worry, I'll speak up for you." His thumb and forefinger made an unmistakable gesture. "Just figure what it's worth and see me an hour after dark. You can bribe your way from the compound if you have to."

"I'll be here," said Dumarest. "Do your best for me and you won't regret it."

At the *Queen of Jaquline* he was met with a scowl.

"Get the hell away from here!" The officer was red-faced, thick-set, impatient. "I've had enough of you thieving swine!

You whine your way aboard, beg for a cheap passage, promise the universe then rob the ship of all you can."

"I want—"

"You'll get a mouthful of broken teeth if you argue! Shen! Hammond! Come and take care of this stinking beggar!"

The third ship was the *Sleethan,* a trader loading crates. Dumarest helped to stack them in the hold and then, when the overseer wasn't looking, slipped past him and into the vessel. The captain was of a type he'd met before.

"Passage?" Kell Erylin rubbed thoughtfully at his jaw. "You can pay?"

Dumarest showed the man some money. "Where are you bound?"

"Zakym." Erylin sucked at his teeth. "How come you helped to load?"

"I needed the exercise." Dumarest met the shrewd eyes. Like all traders the captain was more interested in making a profit than worrying about codes of morality. "And I didn't want to advertise my leaving. Harald's an odd world, Captain, as you know. I've a rooted objection to wearing a collar."

A hint which would explain his appearance, his need to escape. For Erylin it seemed to be enough.

"We leave after dark. Be here an hour before then and—"

"No." Dumarest jingled the coins. "I want to stay aboard, Captain. To settle in, you might say. I'm willing to pay extra for the service."

Erylin held out his hand and frowned as he saw the amount.

"A third in advance," explained Dumarest. "The rest when we're in space. Don't worry, you'll get it."

"If I don't you'll breath vacuum." The captain's tone was as hard as his eyes. Jerking his head he added, "Take cabin number three. Help yourself to food if you want it. Chagney's in the salon."

Chagney was the navigator. He sat sprawled in a chair, foot resting on the table, a cup of basic in his hand. He watched as Dumarest helped himself from the spigot and sipped at the liquid. It was sickly with glucose, thick with protein, flavored with citrus and laced with vitamins. A cup would provide a spaceman with energy for a day.

"Hungry?" The navigator tipped something from a bottle into his own cup. "Here, a little of this gives it more body."

It was brandy and Dumarest tipped the bottle, taking far less than it seemed.

"So you're going to ride with us," said Chagney. "To Zakym. You know it?"

"No."

"A small world deep in the Rift. A crazy place or maybe it's the people who are crazy. We work the area; Zakym, Ieldhara, Frogan, Angku—small profits and plenty of risk. You've ridden traders before?"

"A time or two, yes."

"Then you know how it is." Chagney helped himself to more brandy. Lifting the cup, he said, "A toast, friend. To the afterlife!" His smile was bleak. "You don't think I should drink to the next world? Hell, why not? There's little enough in this one."

And for him less than most. The man was dying, his body ravaged by an internal parasite picked up on some distant world. Soon it would eat its way to his brain but, before that, if Erylin had any sense, the ship would have a new navigator.

"If we can find one." The engineer was a squat man with the body of a toad and a sponge-like face meshed with a tracery of broken veins. "Chagney knows his way around the Rift and we'll have a hard time replacing him. Who wants to work on a trader?"

Usually the ruined, the desperate, those with skills but with reputations long-vanished and with nowhere else to turn. Men willing to take risks with old equipment and worn engines. Scraping a living by sharing in the meager profits. Some, Dumarest had known, were well run and well maintained. The *Sleethan* wasn't one of them.

It was undercrewed; the engineer filling in as handler. There was no steward. The corridor showed signs of dirt and neglect. The decks were scuffed and the air held the sour taint of faulty-conditioners. The cabins matched the rest.

Dumarest closed the door, threw the simple catch and

stripped off the rags and tatters which covered his own clothing. The bunk held a thin mattress, the cabinet was empty, the water from the faucet little more than a trickle into the bowl. He let it run as he stripped then washed himself down, using a sheet from the bunk as both sponge and towel. Dressed he opened the door and looked outside. The corridor was deserted. The cabins to either side were empty but in the one beyond the nearest to the salon he found some clothes hanging in the cabinet. A steward's uniform together with a medical kit containing some basic drugs and antibiotics. With it was a hypogun loaded with quick-time.

Laziness would account for the clothing; the steward, dead or deserted, had left traces which had yet to be disposed of. The kit was standard equipment as was the hypogun. Once on their journey it would be used, the drug injected with a blast of air to slow the metabolism; the chemical magic of quick-time slowing the metabolism so that a normal day would seem a matter of minutes only. A convenience to lessen the tedium of journeys.

Back in his cabin Dumarest settled down on the bunk to wait. He had done all he could. The false trail at the *Ergun* would provide a distraction if one was needed. He wouldn't be missed from the compound. Within an hour now, he would be away from Harald and safe into space.

He dozed a little, waking to the throb of the engines, the thin, high, wailing of the generator as it established the Er-haft field which would send them across the void at a multiple of the speed of light. The wail was ragged, too loud, the audible signal lasting too long before it lifted into the ultra-sonic to be heterodyned into harmlessness.

But the noise didn't matter. The ship was up and away and Dumarest felt himself relax. A moment only, then he tensed as someone knocked on the door.

"Who?"

"Fatshan." The engineer cleared his throat. "Open up, man, it's time for quick-time."

Dumarest frowned, reaching for his knife as, with his other hand, he released the catch. The panel flew open and the engineer cried out at the sight of naked steel.

"No! Don't! I couldn't help it! I—"

He broke off as a hand thrust him to one side. In the corridor now stood a tall figure wearing a hatefully familiar robe.

As Dumarest lifted the naked blade Cyber Broge said, "Drop it! Drop it or I fire!"

The laser in his hand was small, a sleeve-gun, but just as deadly as any other weapon at this range. It could sear and burn and slash like a red-hot blade. Dumarest knew that, if he moved, it would sever both his legs at the knees.

Chapter SEVEN

~~~~~~~~~~~~~~~~

Khaya Taiyuah was a tall, lean man with a hooked nose and sunken eyes which, normally like turgid pools, now blazed with the urgency of his errand.

"Lavinia, we have no choice. Unless Gydapen is stopped he will ruin us all. The Pact must not be broken. If it is then what will become of life as we know it?" Somberly he answered his own question. "War, death, destruction, the ruin of Zakym. The work of our ancestors wasted because of the greed of one man."

He was, she thought, exaggerating, but knew better than to voice the accusation. Taiyuah, like most of his type, was subjected to sudden rages. An introvert, usually uninterested in anything which did not have a bearing on his devotion to breeding a new strain of silk worm, he took little notice of the conduct of others. Now something, a rumor perhaps, had sent him into a state bordering on panic.

Quietly she said, "Gydapen isn't insane, Khaya. He must know what he is doing. Are you sure you have all the facts?"

"A messenger from Fhard Erason gave them to me. I sent him on to Howich Suchong and came here as soon as

I could. Lavinia, you have influence with the man. Stop him before it is too late."

She had, she thought, seen him perhaps a dozen times during the entire course of her life and most of those occasions had been accidental meetings in town when they had both gone to collect delivered consignments. Only twice had he been at a Council meeting. But he had attended the death-rites of her parents—she owed him for that.

"Lavinia—"

"We have time, Khaya. You need rest, food and some wine. A bath too, perhaps. It will relax you. Enjoy it while I arrange matters with Roland."

"You will hurry?"

"I'll waste no time," she promised. "Now do as I say, old friend. And trust me."

Roland was on the upper battlements, standing on the platform, binoculars to his eyes as he swept the distant hills. The magenta sun was high, the violet still barely risen, the air holding a welcome absence of tension. As always, he sensed her presence and, lowering the binoculars, turned, smiling.

"Lavinia!" He sobered as she told him of the visitor and his fears. "And he wants you to do something about it?"

"Yes. Should I?"

"If the Pact is threatened you have no choice. I assume an extraordinary meeting of the Council will be called? If Fhard Erason is sending out word then that will be inevitable. But why didn't he notify you directly?"

A point which hadn't escaped her attention. Slowly she said, "If Erason did send out word. Khaya is old and gets easily confused. Delusia was strong last evening."

"And Khaya keeps much to himself." Roland looked toward the hills, his brows creased with thought. "I'll contact Erason personally and circulate the others. It's possible that Khaya has misjudged the situation. He may not have been meant to contact you. After all, as far as most are concerned, you and Gydapen are close. His interests could be your own. In any case it could be feared that you might warn him or, at least, side with him. It would be a natural assumption."

"But wrong!"

His pleasure was manifest. "It pleases me to hear you say it, my lady."

"I might have to marry the man," she said, ignoring the comment. "But I don't have to like him and I will never side with him if he threatens the Pact." She glanced towards the hills. "What were you studying?"

"The herd we set to browse. Two stallions are vying for supremacy. Here." He handed her the glasses, "To the left of the forked peak and just above the patch of grasses. They could still be there."

They were and she watched, entranced by their sheer, animal perfection as, snorting, they faced each other, hooves pawing the stoney dirt. They would turn and move and weave perhaps for days as their biological needs grew and filled their universe. The urge to procreate would work its magic and each would fight to be the one to impregnate the mares. One would have to yield, running before suffering too serious injuries, forced to wait and build on what he had learned, to prove his mastery and so the right to implant his seed.

Once, perhaps, men had acted in a similar fashion, gathering females under their protection, filling them with new life, multiplying their strength and cunning, their courage and ability to survive. Then only the strong had won the right to continue their line—the weak had perished.

What had happened to ruin that elementary custom?

Where now were the men who, like those distant stallions, would fight to gain and hold what they desired?

"Lavinia?"

She lowered the binoculars, conscious that she had concentrated for too long, become too deeply engrossed with mental imageries and was, perhaps, even now betraying her own, deep-rooted desires. The son of her body would be a man, but where was the man to father him?

Roland? He looked at her now as a dog would look at its master. Gydapen? He owned strength of a kind and it would serve if nothing else could be found. Erason? He was newly bereft of his wife and had sworn never to take another. Suchong, Alcorus, Navolok—all were old with sons too young.

Again she looked through the binoculars towards the hills. The stallions were gone now, racing with the joy of life down the further slopes, perhaps, or engaging in the initial combat-maneuvers which would be a prelude to the real battles to come. She wished she could see them. She wished she were a mare and could watch the savage masculinity of those who fought to possess her. To have men fight and bleed and risk death itself for the sake of the prize she offered.

"Lavinia!"

She lowered the binoculars and turned towards where Roland stood, aware of the urgency of how he had spoken her name, the hunger in his tone. But he was looking towards the far end of the battlement, his head tilting as he looked at the sky.

"We should be making arrangements," he said, mildly. "And the calls had best be made without delay."

She glanced at the suns; they were still far apart but would merge before the afternoon. A bad time for business. And, if they were to reach town safely before night, it was best to waste no more time.

"See to it," she ordered, and handed him the binoculars. "I'll find out what I can from Khaya. As you say he might have imagined the whole thing. If not we can use his raft to transport extra goods to the warehouse."

They left in an hour, both rafts loaded with bales containing ornamented leather articles, carved bone, beads of lambent stones, wood whittled into engrossing shapes; the product of idle hours during winter and times of waiting, the fruit of skilled but primitive artists and those who held a trace of genius.

The agent, a Hausi, kept his features impassive as he studied samples. They would find a market on worlds jaded with machine-production, be used as tools of trade, give pleasure to tourists and children.

"Satisfied with the quality?" Lavinia was sharp, unfairly so. A Hausi did not lie and Jmombota had no need to cheapen the goods. It was proof of her agitation that she had fired the question.

"My lady, I was looking for variety, not doubting the workmanship."

"They are as usual."

"And will find markets, but if I may be so bold to suggest

that a wider range would be more viable—" He broke off, spreading his hands. "The beads, for example, if cut instead of polished they would add to their charm. I could obtain the necessary equipment should you be interested."

"Later." The man meant well—her gain was his greater profit, but she was not to be rushed and had no real interest in the details of trade. The mounts bred by her Family for generations were her real interest. The goods now piled on the floor of the warehouse were a by-product of culled beasts. "Has my consignment arrived yet?"

"No, my lady."

"When?" She anticipated his answer. "You can't be sure. Zakym is a small world and ships have to be sure of making a profit before they call."

"That is so, my lady."

A fact she knew, had always known, and it was useless to rail against the system. It was only a matter of waiting and, in the meantime, there were other things to worry about. Gydapen's apparent madness for one.

He sat in the Council chamber, sprawled in a seat carved of ancient woods and adorned with a motif of beasts and reptiles. A man shorter than herself but with the shoulders of a bull and hands which held a crude beauty in their raw, functional strength. He rose as he saw her, bowing, his eyes bold as he straightened.

"Lavinia Del Belamosk," he said, gravely. "The most lovely object to be found on this world. My lady, I salute you."

"And I you, Gydapen Prabang. My lord, you have us concerned."

"Us?"

"Those of us who, with you, share the rule of this world. Taiyuah, Erason, Alcorus—" She broke off at his smile. "I amuse you?"

"You enchant me, but what have we to do with that list of names?"

"They matter, my lord."

"*You* matter!" He was blunt. "For you, my dear, anything. For them—" he made a gesture as of flicking dust from his sleeve. "But, as you can see, I observe the courtesies. I am here. You are here. The others?"

"Roland is below."

"The Lord Acrae." The corners of his mouth lifted in a quirk. "Of course. And the rest?" He didn't wait for an answer. "You know, Lavinia, I was sitting here thinking of all those who had sat here before and the wise deliberations they must have made and the decisions they arrived at to be handed down through the generations to bind those which followed. Us, my dear. You and I. Are you not weary of the weight of those fetters forged so long ago?"

"Traditions and customs had their purpose. And the Pact—"

"Must not be broken." His interruption was the flash of a naked blade. "Of course. Always it comes to that. The Pact!" His voice was a sneer and, in a moment, he had wiped away his previous gain in her estimation. Strength he might have, but it was the brute strength of an unthinking beast. Against it she would set her own cunning. It, together with the weapons of her sex, might yet prove to be the victor.

"A battle, my dear?" His voice was soft yet hiding venom and she realized that his eyes had been studying her, reading her expression as they had already read the shape of her body beneath her gown. "The prospect excites you?" He took a step towards her and she caught the odor of perfume. A strong, pungent sweetness which masked, but could not wholly disguise another odor, the scent of masculinity which enveloped him like a cloud.

A stallion. A beast in rut.

And she was a mare!

"Lavinia!" Another step and he was close enough to touch her, the weight of his fingers oddly cool against her shoulder. "Next to me you are the strongest person on this world. Think of what we could accomplish if we were together. What couldn't we achieve? You know my feelings. If I were to suggest a union what would you say?"

"I would suggest you waited for the right time and place."

"Do you mock me!"

She saw the sudden anger blaze in face and eyes, the snatched withdrawal of his hand, the backward step which carried him beyond reach. Saw too the vulnerability he had betrayed and, seeing it, sensed her power and potential victory.

"Gydapen you say that, next to you, I am the strongest person on this world. I disagree—you will permit me that?"

Then, as he remained silent, she added, harshly, "Or do you want nothing more than a slave to kiss your boots at your command? Is that what you look for in a wife?"

"A wife?" His eyes cleared. "I—no. No, of course not."

"Good." She glanced around the chamber, seeing the carved heads of long-dead Councillors who watched with blind, indifferent eyes. The living, assembling, would be downstairs. Waiting for all to arrive, perhaps, or for more devious reasons of their own. Well, let them wait. "My Lord Gydapen Prabang, I am hungry. Of your charity, may I be fed?"

The old form of appeal amused him as she had intended it should. It also dissolved the last vestige of his rage and gave him more assurance as to her feelings than he had reason to own.

"Feed you?" His laughter echoed from the beamed and vaulted roof. "My dear, I'll give you the best meal money can buy."

"And the others?"

"To hell with them! They can wait!"

Wait as viands were carefully selected and prepared, cooked to stringent standards, dressed and blended with expensive oils and spices, served with deference and with appropriate wines. A succession of dishes culled from a score of worlds. Specialties costing more than an ordinary worker could accumulate in half a year of toil.

Lavinia speared a morsel and tasted sweetness, bit into crispness, swallowed a savory pulp tantalizing in varying flavors. Another followed as different as the first, more, a host of morsels each blending with the other, triggering barely remembered incidents of past happinessess.

Warmth, born in her stomach, spread to her thighs, her breasts, her loins.

Her glass was empty and a servant poured at her host's command. Vapors rose from the sparkling fluid, drifting clouds of tantalizing sweetness which held something of the emerald fluid and hinted of mint and ice and chilled lavender.

"To us, my dear." Gydapen lifted his own goblet. "To our future!"

"To joy," she responded with ambiguity. "To fulfillment."

They drank and, if he anticipated more than was meant by the words, that was his loss and her victory. With him always it would be a battle. As they lowered their goblets the deep throb of the curfew gong sent little sympathetic tintinnabulations from the engraved crystal.

"Night." Gydapen's tone was sour. "And now the Sungari come into their own."

"Night." She touched the rim of her goblet as, again, the gong throbbed its warning. "I must thank you, my lord, for having fed me so well."

"Of my charity?"

"Of your charity." She smiled as if they shared a private joke. Then, growing serious, she said, "You know, the old forms have meaning. The implicit courtesy, for example, and the reminder that to be polite, even to the deprived, is to be civilized. I asked you to feed me and you did and for that I thanked you. We find it amusing, but what if I had been starving? Had I demanded you would have refused and then, in order to survive, I would have tried to take by force what you refused to give me. In which case I would have, most probably, died."

"Not you, Lavinia."

"Because you consider me to be attractive?"

"Because you are rare—a woman with intelligence and a man's ability to get your own way."

"And those things are rare?" She thought for a moment, "On Zakym, perhaps, but on other worlds? You have travelled, Gydapen. So has Roland. He tells me that, on some worlds, women are equal in all respects to men. Have you found it so?"

"It is against nature."

"It is?" She frowned, sensing more than an unthinking rebuttal and wondering why an otherwise intelligent man should have affirmed such nonsense. Had he been hurt on his travels? Meeting a woman who had beaten him at his own game? Who had mocked him and held him to scorn? If so she must be careful. Whatever Gydapen lacked it was not physical strength. In an actual fight he could break her bones and, from what she remembered of the rage which had distorted his face, he would, given cause. "Well, perhaps you are right. In any case what true woman would ever want a man as weak as herself?"

For answer he flicked the edge of his goblet with a nail and, as the thin, high chime began to fade, said, "I'll be blunt, Lavinia. I want you. I think you know it."

"You want me," she said, dryly. "As what and for how long?"

"As wife."

"I would accept nothing less."

"I would offer nothing less." His eyes met her own, hard, direct. "I have no time for games. Unite with me and, in time, our children could rule this world. Think about it."

She knew better than to jest. Returning his stare she said, with sincerity, "You have done me honor, my lord. For this I thank you."

And, if no word of love had been spoken, what of that? Did animals prate of romance when locked in the compulsion to procreate? Did babies need soft words and gentle hands in order to be conceived? She was a Lady of Zakym, not a servant girl with a too-large imagination and a too-limited awareness of reality. Gydapen had offered her power and prestige, security for her people and a father for her children. Could any man offer more?

Then why did she continue to hesitate? Why, when the aphrodisical qualities of the food and wine warmed her loins, did she continue to remain aloof?

Questions the carved figures on the stairs couldn't answer. Nor did the wooden heads in the Council chamber. Even the living remained silent, the silence a mute reproach for having being kept waiting.

Gydapen broke it. Plumping into his seat he said, "Well, you asked me to come and I am here."

Erason held the chair. Coldly he said, "The formalities must be observed. First an apology for the wilful insult to the Council. "Then—"

"To hell with that!" The slap of Gydapen's hand was a meaty thud rising from the table. "Get on with it or I leave."

Alcorus cleared his throat. Old, withered, he hated displays of violence. Hated, not feared, two dead men killed in a formal duel proved that.

"I'll make this short Lord Prabang. I've heard that you intend to break the Pact. Is that true?"

"And if it is?"

"I ask for the last time." The dry tones held contempt. "Is it true?"

"No." Gydapen looked around as relief made an audible rustle as clothing shifted on relaxing bodies. "I have no intention of actually breaking the Pact. But it can be altered. Adjustment can be made."

"You split hairs, my lord!"

"I'm giving you the truth, Alorcus." Gydapen returned the old man's glare. "There are valuable minerals on my lands. I intend to obtain them. That is all."

"And what of the Pact?" Navolok leaned forward in his chair. "Do you intend to defy the Sungari?"

"I've explained that."

"No." Suchong made a curt gesture. "You have done nothing of the kind. You, like all of us, have certain designated areas for mining. Now you say that you intend to extend your area of operations. This is a direct contravention of the Pact."

"It has already been contravened."

"By whom? The Sungari? How? When?"

"You want proof?"

"I demand it!" Alcorus returned to the attack. "It is essential. Without evidence I refused to accept your testimony."

"You dare to call me a liar!"

"Do you take us for fools?" With an effort Alcorus restrained his anger. "Do you ask us to destroy our heritage on your unsupported word? If the Pact has been broken then we must know how and where and in what manner. Accidents have happened before but the Pact has been maintained. It will still be maintained with good intent on both sides. But if you, or anyone, deliberately breaks if for reasons of selfish greed then the full weight of this Council will be turned against him. I call for a vote!"

Dutifully Lavinia raised her hand and, with surprise, noted that Gydapen also voted in favor. A cynical gesture or a genuine desire to keep the peace? A cunning move in order to gain time? It was possible and she wondered who had first spread the rumor. Gydapen himself, perhaps, it would fit his nature. To cry wolf again and again so that when he really did set to work who would believe it?

The Council dissolved in apparent concord, the members taking underground passages to their various places of accomodation. Lavinia made certain that Gydapen should not claim her, an act made simple by his own apparent lack of interest; another cunning move on his part, perhaps, or a demonstration of calculated patience. The average woman would have been piqued by such an apparent affront and eager to prove the worth of her attraction.

Roland pursed his lips when, later in her room, she mentioned it.

"Gydapen is cunning, Lavinia. Never make the mistake of underestimating him."

"I don't intend to."

"I watched him in the Council chamber. His rage—did you notice how artificial it was? And he seemed to want to goad certain members. The vote, of course, was a farce."

"But, even so, what could he do against us?"

The room was small; one in a relatively inexpensive hotel, the panelling uncarved, the wooden floor graced only with a thin rug. The window, now firmly shuttered, was of small panes of colored glass, reflections from the lamp filling it with a jig-saw of multicolored hues which touched Roland's hair and sharpened his features.

Quietly he said, "The wrong question, my dear. You should ask, what can we do against him should he choose to go his own way?"

"He wouldn't dare!"

"Why not?" He turned and now his face, sharper than before, held a sagging weariness. "Like me he's been to other worlds. He knows how limited Zakym can be. With money the galaxy is waiting. Worlds without number, races, civilizations, climates, how to even begin to tell of their variety? And he has no cause to love this planet. If it came to it he would ruin it and leave, smiling, revelling in his revenge."

She said, with quick understanding, "Me?"

"You could be the last straw. He wants you. I do not say he loves you; personally I think the man incapable of anything aside from self-love. You would be an acquisition. An excuse if you rejected him."

"No!" She refused to accept the burden. "No, Roland! You can't place the fate of this world on my shoulders! I won't have it!"

He made no answer, just stood watching her, waiting as the moments dragged past and the obvious came to stand before her and smile with its fleshless jaws.

What she wanted was no longer of importance—like it or not she had no choice.

Chapter EIGHT

No ship traversing space was ever truly silent, always, if it lived, there was sound. Small noises, vibrations carried by the structure, the tap of a boot against metal, the muted sussuration of voices, the quiver of the generators and the soft, near-inaudible drone of the Erhaft field itself. A drone which was more of a vibration than actual noise, a thing which could be felt with the tips of sensitive fingers. On a good vessel with efficient padding such noises were unobtrusive, a background murmur which provided comfort rather than distraction, a sense of life in a sterile void, but the *Sleethan* was far from new and the sounds were loud. But not loud enough to drown the even modulation of Cyber Broge.

"You displayed wisdom. You knew that I would not have hesitated to fire."

Dumarest said, dryly, "And broken your command not to risk my life?"

"I have skill in medical matters. The stumps would have been seared by the beam and blood-loss avoided. There would have been relatively little shock. Tourniquets could have been applied and other precautions taken. You would have been in no danger of losing your life."

"And yet you couldn't be certain of that?"

"Nothing can be absolutely guaranteed," admitted the cyber. "Always there is the possibility of the unknown affecting any prediction. Yet, had you left me no choice, I would have taken the risk."

A fact Dumarest had known. He could have hurled the knife and, perhaps, taken the man's life, but he would have fallen beneath the beam and, falling, died.

Also, somewhere, the man's acolyte would have been on watch.

Was still on watch.

Dumarest had seen him after he had dropped the knife and obeyed the cyber's orders. Deft hands had removed his boots, his tunic, leaving him dressed only in his pants. His hands had been cuffed behind him and, once on the cot, his ankles had been manacled to the structure of the bed. He could sit upright, turn from side to side, could even throw himself awkwardly to the floor. But it was impossible to leave the bunk.

A prisoner, he could only wait.

Wait and watch and plan. To be ready at all times to take advantage of any opportunity which might come. To mask the alertness by a seeming, numb acceptance of his fate. To use a man's weakness against himself.

Broge was young, inexperienced, sent to Harald because it was a world of relative unimportance and would serve to train him in the extension of his instilled attributes. A man who, while not capable of true emotion, could enjoy the pleasure of mental achievement. And he had succeeded in gaining the one man the Cyclan wanted most of all.

"You were clever," said Dumarest. "How did you know where I would be?"

"The clues were obvious. The stolen clothing, rubbish, perhaps, but good enough to disguise your own garments. The rain helped and you probably waited in the market until dark. Then where could you hide without question? The prediction that you would choose Lowtown was high. You would be on the field, close to vessels, and you would have money for passage should the opportunity present itself."

He knew everything. To walk into Lowtown had been simple, who would think a man would voluntarily want to stay in such a stinking hell? Men were counted out but rarely counted in. To join a party in the gloom, to merge into the shadows, to wait.

"How did you know where to look for me? Only the woman knew I was at the old man's."

And she would have told the cyber when he asked, of course, and his absence when her home was searched would have confirmed the prediction as to where he would be found. It was impossible to blame her; on Harald a good situation was something to be valued. The rest was elementary, the captain of the *Sleethan,* warned, would have sent word.

"I must admit that I was puzzled by the ease of your capture," said Broge. "I was given to understand that you had remarkable powers of eluding authority. It seems incredible that you remained at large for so long."

"Luck," said Dumarest. "I had a lot of luck."

Which had turned bad on Harald. An hour, maybe, would have done it. A day, certainly. If he could have gained a passage before the cyber had been informed—but no ships had been at the field and, once in Lowtown, he could only wait.

Even then, if Erylin had been honest—but to ask that of his kind was to ask too much. The captain, bribed, would not have hesitated.

Dumarest said, "Listen, you don't need me. I'm willing to cooperate with you. I'll tell you the secret you're looking for and, in return, you let me go. Just give me my boots."

"You have the secret hidden in your boots?"

"I—never mind that. You must know why the Cyclan want me. Well, you can take them what they want. I'll write it down if—" Dumarest jerked at his manacled wrists. "What's the matter with you? Are all you people thieves?"

"You are the thief. You stole the secret from the Cyclan. We only want to recover what is rightfully ours."

An error, the secret had been stolen by Brasque and passed by him to Kalin who, in turn, had given it to Dumarest. A correction he didn't make as, again, he tugged at his wrists. An act, there could be no escape from the clamping metal, but a man who would waste effort on a useless pursuit would merit the scorn of the cyber and a man held in scorn is generally underestimated.

A knock and, at the cyber's invitation, the door opened and Chagney stood just within the cabin. He looked blankly at Dumarest and swayed a little, lifting a hand to support himself, the fingers thin, the knuckles swollen against the jamb.

"The captain wants to know the new destination. You said—"

"You are bound at present for Zakym?"

"Yes. It's on the edge of the Rift. We've a cargo and can pick up stuff for delivery to Koyan."

"Alter course for Jalong. Full recompense will be made on arrival together with the promised bonus." Then, as the navigator made no attempt to shift his position, the cyber added, "Well?"

"Jalong. You sure?"

"Yes."

"It's beyond the Rift. You know that?"

"I know it." Broge looked steadily at the navigator. "Are you ill?"

"He's drunk," said Dumarest. "He couldn't plot an unfamiliar course to save his life. Anyway, we'll never reach Jalong in this wreck. The generators are shot to hell, can't you hear them? Try it and we'll all end up as dust in the Rift."

"The probability of that is six point seven per cent," said Broge evenly. "Low as you will admit. Once on Jalong you will be transhipped to a vessel which will take you to your final destination."

Final in more ways than one. Dumarest leaned back against the bulkhead as Broge rose and led Chagney back to the control room. Alone his face lost its vacuous expression as he anticipated the future. It didn't take a cyber's skill to predict just what would happen. First he'd be held in a security impossible to achieve on the *Sleethan*. There would be guards and drugs and preliminary interrogations. Later would come electronic probes to quest his brain, pain to stimulate his memory, tests to determine the truth, more to eliminate the possibility of error. Then, finally, when no longer human, he would be disposed of as unwanted rubbish.

It would be done without hate and without mercy. The events of the past would have no meaning for those who would have him in their charge. The Cyclan wasted no time on recriminations or revenge. He would be nothing more to them than a receptacle holding the one thing they had determined to regain.

The correct sequence of the fifteen biological molecular units forming the affinity twin.

An artificial symbiote developed by the Cyclan in a secret laboratory and stolen from them by the dedicated genius of one man. Brasque was long dead now as was Kalin and he had destroyed the data before taking the secret or had left false information behind. The details didn't matter, the fact that the affinity twin still existed did.

Injected into the bloodstream it nestled at the base of the cortex and became intermeshed with the entire sensory and nervous systems. The brain hosting the submissive half of the organism would become a literal extension of the dominant part. Each move, all sensation, all mobility would be instantaneously transmitted. In effect it gave the host containing the dominant half a new body.

It offered a bribe impossible to resist.

An old man could become young again, enjoying to the full the senses of a virile, healthy body. A harridan could see her beauty reflected in the eyes of her admirers. The hopelssly crippled and hideously diseased would be cured, their minds released from the rotting prison of their flesh.

It would give the Cyclan the complete and utter domination of the galaxy.

The mind and intelligence of a cyber would reside in every ruler and person of influence and power. They would become marionettes moving to the dictates of their masters. Slaves such as had never been seen before, mere extensions of those who wore the scarlet robe.

They would rediscover the secret in time, but the possible combinations of the fifteen units ran into the millions and, even if it were possible to test one combination every second, to check them all would take more than four thousand years.

Dumarest could cut that time down to a matter of days.

The reason they hunted him from world to world. Had hunted him. Luck alone had saved him until now. Luck and his own shrewdness, his instinctive awareness of danger. An awareness which had been blunted in his consuming desire to discover the coordinates of Earth.

Again he tested the manacles around his wrists. They were locked tight but there was a little slack in the connecting chain, enough to allow of a little free movement. He slid his hands far to one side, gripped his belt and tugged. It moved a little, jammed, moved again as, sweating, he jiggled the strap. The buckle slid through a loop, struck again, yielded only when his arms were burning with strain.

He froze as a gust of air touched his face. He saw nothing and the door had not apparently opened or closed, but the impact of the minor breeze was real. A moment and the door opened and Chagney entered the cabin. He stood, swaying, his eyes glazed, his breath a noisome foulness.

"No good." He muttered. "No good."

"What's wrong? The cyber?"

"The red swine. Said I didn't know my trade. I'd plotted the course and he found an error. So what's in a small error? We can correct as we go, can't we?"

"Is he navigating?"

"No." Chagney swayed again and almost fell. "I'm doing that. I'm the navigator and it's my job. I insisted. The captain's checking my figures, that's all."

And the cyber would check again. He didn't have to be a navigator, Erylin would take care of that, every captain had schooling in the basics if nothing else. Chagney, as the man dimly realized, had been declared incompetent.

An ally, perhaps? Aggrieved he might be willing to help. Dumarest said, "These manacles are tearing my arms off. Can you ease them a little?"

"No." The navigator shook his head. "No key," he explained. "The acolyte has that and he's riding Middle."

Space terminology for anyone travelling under normal time. For him the journey would be a grinding tedium but, living at a normal rate while the others were slowed by quick-time, he would make a perfect guard. Even if Dumarest managed to escape he would stand no chance. And he was being watched, the puff of air proved that; the acolyte had looked into the cabin, seen all was well and had left again before Dumarest could react.

An invisible guardian added to the rest—the cyber was taking no chances.

Dumarest eased himself up in order to lean his back against the bulkhead. He winced, muttered, swore as he moved again. Chagney watched with dull interest; unaware of the hidden fingers which tore at the buckle of the belt now resting against Dumarest's kidneys.

"What they want you for? The Cyclan, I mean, you're valuable to them, right?"

The voice was still slurred but the eyes had lost some of their glaze. Somehow his pride had been stung or his greed wakened and he was trying to learn what he could. A mistake on the cyber's part, another to add to the rest and Dumarest's only chance. He took it, quickly, before the door could be sealed and he was isolated.

"I've got something they want," he said quickly. "The coordinates where it is buried. A smart man could make himself a fortune, but I wasn't smart enough. Listen, you help me and I'll tell you where it is."

He paused, waiting as moments dragged, fighting the tension which mounted within him. The seed had been sown but it was slow to take root. The diseased brain could only ponder what had been said.

And, to say more at this time, would be a mistake.

Chagney sucked at his lips. "What is it? This stuff you buried?"

"I didn't bury it. It's a ship which crashed on Heida. You know it? The hold was stuffed with equipment for the mines but there was something else carried in the captain's cabin. A strongbox filled with gems. They were meant as a bribe to the Magnate from the Cyclan. He didn't get them and they had to pay twice. Now they want the gems."

"And you know where they are?"

Dumarest said, "Help me ease these damned cuffs. They're tearing the skin."

"The gems—"

"To hell with the gems. Help ease these cuffs."

The navigator took one step forward then paused. He

blinked and ran the tip of his tongue over cracked and scaled lips. He said, slowly, "These gems—are you conning me?"

"How much is the cyber paying as recompense? How large a bonus are you getting? Sure, I'm conning you. Forget it."

Dumarest turned, scowling, the nail of his thumb probing at metal. The buckle was in reverse, unseen, he could only operate by touch and, for safety, the thing wasn't easy to open. It yielded as Chagney took another step towards him.

"The gems? How much?"

"If you know Heida then you know the Magnate. He lives high. A man like that can't be bought cheap. There's enough to keep the both of us in luxury for life." Dumarest hardened his voice. "The both of us, understand?"

"But—"

"I'll delay the Cyclan. You get there first and find the stuff. Hide it and wait. I'll join you as soon as I can. On—where? Where shall we meet?" Dumarest didn't have to pretend urgency. Beneath his fingers the buckle had parted and the small, metal tube it had contained now was in his hands. It contained two syringes one colored red, the other green. They contained the affinity twin, the subjective with a reversed last component. But how to tell which from which?

"Koyan," said Chagney. "I like Koyan. I've got friends there. I'll wait for you on Koyan."

"Where? How will I locate you?"

"I'll be at the best hotel. Now how do I find the gems?"

If they existed he would take them all, but his greed had served its purpose. Now, quickly, before the chance was lost. The only chance he would get. But which was the red syringe?

As he struggled to remember their original location in the tube, the shift of position of both buckle and container, and which now occupied what position, Dumarest said, "We had a deal. Come closer. Ease these damned cuffs."

"The coordinates—"

"You want everyone to hear. Bend down your ear to my mouth. Hurry, damn you. Hurry!"

He caught the stench of foul breath in his nostrils as the navigator obeyed. Heard the rasp of air in wheezing lungs and heard, too, the pad of feet down the corridor outside. The cyber returning?

A scaled cheek touched his own, an ear moving to halt opposite his mouth, haired, grimed with dirt and wax. Dumarest muttered words, figures, giving an imagined position, instructions, lies. Holding the other's attention as he strained against his bonds, fingers slimed with sweat, muscles burning as he fought to hold the syringe. Fingers touched his arms, moved down to his wrists, hesitated.

"Lower," said Dumarest. "Lower, grab those manacles and pull. Move, damn you! Hurry!"

"Someone's coming."

Had arrived, the footsteps halting beyond the cabin opening, moving forward as, with a lunge, Dumarest reared, stabbing upwards with the syringe, feeling the point strike against a boney wrist, slip, drive home as he reared again, pain lancing from torn ligaments in back and shoulders.

"What the hell!" Chagney swore and tried to jerk free his arms. Dumarest threw back his weight, imprisoning them between his shoulders and the bulkhead, releasing his grip on the syringe and turning the other so that the needle rested against the artery on the inside of his wrist. A moment he paused—if he had guessed wrong this would be the last action he would ever take and then, as Broge crossed the cabin towards the bunk, he drove the instrument into his flesh.

Chapter NINE

There was a blur, a timeless moment as if the very universe had stopped, then came light and sound and a voice.

"What are you doing here? My orders were plain. This man is to remain in isolation."

The cyber, his tones even, only the words holding an implicit threat. But the words were fuzzed, harmonics lost, the drone of a robot rather than the trained modulation of his class.

"Did you hear me? Step back away from the prisoner. Leave this cabin and do not return. There will be penalties if you do not obey."

Dumarest sucked in his breath and felt a liquid gurgling in his chest. Before him he could see the metal of the cabin; the join where bulkhead met hull. Lower a shape sat slumped in the corner, arms behind the chest, chin pressed against his own torso.

With a jerk he freed the wrists which were trapped between the figure and the metal. A spot of red caught his eye, a small tube hanging from a needle buried in his wrist and he snatched it, pulling it free, coughing, lifting a hand to his mouth and hiding the thing beneath his tongue.

One found and hidden but the other?

He heard the soggy rasp as of clothing; bare flesh sliding over the metal bulkhead as the figure on the bed toppled to one side. He caught it, found the other syringe, coughed again and finally turned to face the cyber.

"I'll," he said. "I heard him cry out and looked inside and he was ill. I think he's fainted or something."

"Please leave immediately."

"I could help, maybe?"

"That will not be necessary." Broge's hand lifted towards his sleeve, the laser clipped to his wrist. "I shall not ask you again."

The man should die, had to die, executed if for no other reason than that he had ordered the death of an old and harmless man, but not yet. The acolyte had to be taken care of first and there were other things which needed to be done.

How to use this new body for one.

Dumarest sagged as he stepped into the corridor, not acting, unable to master the reluctance of the flesh he now wore. The wall was cool against his fevered skin and he leaned against it, feeling the painful pulsation of his lungs, the liquid gurgling, the rasp of breath, the aches and torments, the agony of rotting tissue.

Chagney was dying.

That he had known, but had been unable to guess just how bad the man had been. The disease had progressed too far, alcohol alone had helped to numb the pain and provide the energy for motivation. Bleakly Dumarest looked at the lights, frowning as his eyes refused to focus. His hearing was impaired, his sight, in his mouth rested foulness, his skin felt like abrasive paper and, like little pits of fire, various glands signaled breakdown and inner decay.

"Chagney!" A man came into sight following his voice. Fatshan, the engineer, a steaming cup of basic in one hand, a bottle in the other. "Man, you look like hell! Here, get this down, you need it."

Dumarest reached for the bottle, missed, his hand closing on empty air. He tried again, more slowly this time, shaken by his lack of coordination. As a cripple had to watch every step so he would have to watch every move.

"Thanks." The brandy stung the raw tissues of the lower region of his throat, pain which helped to wash away other pain, the spirit lending him strength. In the pit of his stomach a small fire sprang into life, warming with its comfort.

As again he gulped at the bottle Fatshan said, "Take it easy, man. You still have work to do."

"Like hell I have." Dumarest wiped the back of his hand across his mouth, saw the other's expression and realized he had made a mistake. Chagney, diseased though he was could have retained some elements of a near-forgotten culture. "I can't worry any more," he said. "Not about the ship, not about you, not anything. Erylin's got himself a new navigator. Well, if that's the way he wants it—" Again he lifted the bottle to his mouth, keeping his lips closed and only pretending to drink.

"You're a fool, " said the engineer. "The Old Man still needs you. With your share of the profits you can get fixed up. Regrafts, maybe, a spell in an amniotic tank, medical aid at least. Why throw it all away?" His voice dropped a little. "Remember Eunice? She'll be waiting when we reach Koyan. Think of the pleasure she can give. Say, what did happen the last time we were there? You know when she—"

Knowledge he didn't have. Dumarest snapped, "Shut up!"

"What?"

"Keep your stinking nose out of my business!"

The reaction was immediate. The engineer scowled, lifted clenched fists and came forward intent on punishment. Dumarest tried to back, felt the slowness of his reflexes and realized that, in his present condition, he stood no chance. He threw himself to one side, hands lifted, brandy spilling from the bottle to the deck.

"No! Don't hit me! I didn't mean anything! Please! It's my head! My head!"

The engineer lowered his fists.

"What the hell's come over you? You might be weak but you always had guts. Now you don't seem to be the same man. That thing hit your brain? Is that it?"

Dumarest sucked in his breath, teeth rattling on glass as he lifted the bottle. The man had touched on something dangerous. Repeated and heard by the cyber it could be fatal.

"God, I feel queer. Things keep getting mixed up. I

thought you were—well, never mind. That time on Koyan. Eunice. She—"

"Forget it." The engineer waved a hand. He looked at the mess on the deck where he'd dropped the cup of basic and shrugged. "More work."

"I'll take care of it."

"Let it lie. Who the hell cares? You'd better get some rest and get into condition. The Old Man's rusty when it comes to navigation and that cyber's no good. Only his money." He chuckled. "That we can use."

For things best left to the imagination but Dumarest wasn't concerned. Checking the cabins he found one which held some books, a scatter of clothing. The books were navigational tables, the clothing fitted the body he now wore. Closing the door he examined it.

Thin, waste, the skin scaled and blotched, a cluster of sores, grime in the pores.

It needed a bath. It lacked any medication. It was an envelope which had seen too many vicissitudes. And in it, somewhere, was housed the original life.

It was below the level of consciousness, a brain trapped in a small, enclosed world, the ego, the individual negated into a formless, timeless region. Yet not all had been eradicated. Sitting, leaning back, relaxing the body while he concentrated on the mind, Dumarest caught odd fragments of distorted memory, items of information he hadn't previously known.

The art of navigation, he felt, was almost at his fingertips. Study it for a while and all would be clear. Jalong—how best to reach Jalong? The Rift held dangers best avoided so head first toward Ystallephra and then alter course to—yes. It was all so obvious.

As was the need for haste.

Dumarest rose and took several deep breaths. It was hard to remember that he wasn't really in this body but lying slumped in apparent unconsciousness in the cyber's cabin. If that body was destroyed then he would die. If Chagney should die then he would wake in his own form. What he now experienced was a total affinity but not a complete transfer. The difference meant survival.

The passage was deserted as far as he could see. So was

the salon. Visible evidence meant nothing, the acolyte could be anywhere, but, living at the normal rate as he was, tiredness would be a problem. He would have to snatch rest or use drugs and either would demand his attention at times.

The steward's cabin was as he remembered it, the clothing a mute testimony of the man who had once occupied the space. The medical kit was untouched. The hypogun lay where the engineer had tossed it after injecting them all with quick-time. All aside from the acolyte, of course, to forget that was to invite destruction.

Lifting the hypogun Dumarest checked it, aimed it at his throat and pulled the trigger.

The air-blast made a sharp hiss, the drug blasted into his bloodstream was unnoticeable but, as the sound of the blast died, the neutralizer took effect.

The lights flickered a little. Sounds changed. Time altered as his metabolism speeded back to its normal rate. Those still under the influence of quick-time became statues.

Broge was in his cabin, stooped over the limp figure on the bunk, a thin blade poised over a figure, blood on the needle-poing steel and blood like a ruby at the point where it had been thrust beneath a nail.

He didn't turn as Dumarest stepped forward. He stayed immobile as the stiletto-like blade was taken from his hand. He did nothing as it thrust itself into the soft place behind an ear, sliding upwards into the brain, the wound closing as it was withdrawn. Poetic justice, death neatly and swiftly delivered and a step taken towards safety.

Without moving Dumarest looked around. His knife, tunic and boots must be somewhere else, logically in the cabin held by the acolyte. Which would place it toward the rear of the passage towards the engine room. As the cyber fell with a soft thud to the floor he stepped from the cabin.

And almost died.

Luck saved him. Luck and the quick recognition of the situation, an ability unaffected by the diseased body. A flicker of movement where no movement should be. A stir—and he froze as the acolyte stepped from a cabin and came towards him.

He looked tired, body slumped with fatigue, shoulders

rounded, head bent, feet dragging. For days now, normal time, he had stayed awake. Drugs had given him a little respite and, perhaps, training had helped a little but no creature, man or emotionless machine, using oxygen as a basic form of energy could deny nature to the extent of rejecting sleep.

Yet, even so, he was aware and alert enough to be suspicious. Dumarest he would have recognized and taken immediate action. The navigator was just a part of the ship. A man who, perhaps, had been summoned by his master for consultation. And one obviously under the influence of quick-time.

It was far from easy. Dumarest stood, immobile, his eyes open, the balls stinging with the need of moisture. His chest ached and his lungs craved air as he waited, not trusting his reflexes, knowing only that he was weak and ill and must kill without mistake or hesitation.

Kill without mercy. Kill to be safe. Kill to survive.

The acolyte reached the cabin, frowned at the open door, halted as he glanced inside.

"Master!"

He spun as Dumarest moved, the action alone being enough to trigger his alarm. The thin sliver of steel aimed at his throat slashed across the face instead, ripping a furrow from the ear and through an eye, blinding, sending blood to pour over the cheek.

A wound which would have caused a normal youth to scream with pain, to back, to be thrown off-guard.

Dumarest grunted as he came in to the attack, one hand lifted, the other snatching at the weapon. The thin blade was almost useless; without weight or balance, too fragile to stab it was good only to slash. Shallow wounds which could hurt but not kill. And to a servant of the Cyclan pain was a stranger.

Dodging the blade he lifted his hand, the laser firing, chipped paint flaring on the cabin wall as, throwing himself down, Dumarest avoided the beam. He rolled as the acolyte fired again, feeling the burn as it hit his left thigh, feeling too the cloth of the scarlet robe spread over the dead body on the floor.

The cyber whom the acolyte didn't know was dead. His

master whom he was sworn to protect with his life. To fire again was to risk hitting the sprawled figure. It was better to wait, to back a little, weapon ready in case of need but aimed safely away.

"The knife," he said. "Drop it." Then, as Dumarest obeyed. "Now up on your feet. Up."

Dumarest fumbled, moved, hands gripping the cyber's dead arm, fingers questing for the laser beneath the wide sleeve. He found it, found the trigger, turning the entire arm towards the acolyte in a grotesque gesture from the dead, as too late, the youth recognized the truth.

He swayed a little, his remaining eye turning into a charred hole in the contours of his face, blood masking his cheek, dripping, falling as he fell to coat the floor with a liquid crimson.

A pool of blood which grew as Dumarest's own wound pumped away his life.

He ripped away the material from the injured thigh, thrust a thumb above the wound where the great artery pulsed and, with the remaining hand and his teeth, ripped a strip of fabric from the cyber's robe. Knotted, twisted into place, it made a crude but efficient tourniquet. Rising, Dumarest staggered and almost fell.

It wasn't just the wound. The beam had missed the bone and he had stanched the blood, but too much had been lost already and he was too weak. His heart pounded like a bursting engine and the lights appeared to dim as he fought for air. The tips of his fingers felt cold and, he knew, death was close.

Too close and too soon. He fought it, gritting his teeth, concentrating on the single act of breathing and, slowly, the immediate danger passed.

Only the impossible remained.

The dead had to be disposed of, the cabin cleaned and other matters taken care of. It would need strength and time—but now, at least, he had won some time.

Time in which to clean himself and don fresh clothing. To force himself to drink three cups of basic. To search the medical kit for appropriate drugs.

Fatshan looked up from his console as Dumarest entered the engine room. He scowled. "What do you want?"

"To apologise." Dumarest held out a bottle and a pair of glasses. "I was a fool and I'm making no excuses but, at times, I don't know which way to turn. I'm dying and we both know it. I haven't a friend in the universe aside from you. Let's drink to old times."

"You're crazy!"

"Yes. I'm not arguing. I deserve all you want to hand out. But, for now, let's drink to the past." Dumarest poured neat brandy into the glasses. "To health and happiness. To the next world." A pause then, "To death and what comes after."

"Cut it out!" Fatshan glared over the rim of his glass. "Your toasts give me the creeps at times. Death'll come when it's ready, until then let's enjoy life."

"I'll drink to that!"

Dumarest lifted his glass, watched as the other swallowed the contents of his own at a gulp. Refilling the container he handed it back, coughed, wiped his lips and sipped at his brandy.

As it touched his lips the engineer sighed and collapsed, a victim of the drug Dumarest had given him. He would sleep for a while, wake with a sense of well-being and, while he slept, the field was clear in which to work.

Dumarest fired a charge of neutralizer into his bloodstream and felt the surge and pulse of a disturbed metabolism threaten his awareness. Too free a use of the drugs was dangerous but he had no choice. To risk the side effects was a gamble he had to take.

Back in the cabin nothing had changed. He took the youth first, rolling the body on to a sheet, fastening it, rising to grip the corners and drag it down the passage into the engine room and through into the hold. A port took it, rotating so as to hurl it into the void. The cyber followed, his extra weight robbing Dumarest of strength so that he leaned against a crate, sweat dripping to stain the wood.

Cleaning the cabin came next, swabs soaked in blood added to a pile and all thrown out to join the corpses.

The keys of the manacles had been on the acolyte. Dumarest used them to free his body. His knife, boots and tunic were in the place he'd suspected and he dressed the limp figure. Again using the sheet he dragged it down to the cargo hold.

A way to escape. To beat the Cyclan. The only way.

The lid of a crate lifted to reveal a mass of objects wrapped in plastic; stubby machine rifles thickly protected with grease. Dumarest weighed one in his hand, replaced it and resealed the crate. Another, differently marked, revealed bags containing seeds, tubers, fibrous masses, jelly-like pastes—all relatively light and bulky. Half of them went through the port into the void.

Into the space they'd taken he heaved his limp and unconscious body.

The effort almost killed him so that, for a long time, he leaned against the crate, gasping, fighting for breath, feeling as if his heart had burst and had drenched his guts with blood. Drugs helped, lessening the pain as he fired them into his throat, more followed to give a brief span of false energy for which he would pay later.

But it was almost over.

He studied the crate when it was sealed. No trace could be seen of it ever having been opened. No one would have reason to look.

No one—now that the cyber was dead.

And now, at last, he could rest. To go to his cabin, to lie on the bunk, to watch as the ceiling dimmed and to drift into an endless sea of confused memories all shattered as Fatshan came bursting into the cabin.

He had a cup of basic in his hand, the thick liquid laced with brandy and, as Dumarest sipped, he talked.

"The craziest thing. Gone—the lot of them. Not a trace. Not even of the acolyte. The Old Man and me went Middle and searched the ship all over. Nothing."

Dumarest said, "Slow down. What are you talking about?" He frowned as the engineer explained. "Vanished? You mean they've all vanished?"

"Yes."

"But how? An emergency sac?"

"None are missing and, anyway, who in their right mind would bale out unless they had to?" Fatshan rubbed at his scalp. "I've been in space over thirty years and I've never bumped into anything like this. I can't see how it could have happened. I just can't."

"But it did?"

"It did." The engineer shook his head. "I'm not joking, but it's crazy."

"A fight," said Dumarest. "The prisoner, Dumarest, could have broken free somehow and killed the cyber. He could have been dragging him to the port when the acolyte found him. They had a fight and, somehow, all went through the port."

"You believe that?"

"Maybe the acolyte killed Dumarest and was evicted as a punishment. Then the cyber, unable to admit failure, followed." Then, as the engineer dubiously shook his head, he snapped, "How the hell do I know what happened? I'm guessing, I'll admit it, but do you have a better explanation?"

"No," admitted Fatshan. "And neither does the captain."

He was in the salon, pacing the floor, frowning, kicking at the table as he passed. His frown deepened as he saw Dumarest enter with the engineer. Deliberately he sniffed at the air.

"Brandy. I've told you before about drinking on duty."

"I didn't think I was on duty," said Dumarest. "The cyber had taken over. You and he didn't need me—or so I understood. Anyway, what's the harm in a drink?"

"He needs it, Captain." The engineer coughed. "His trouble, you know. It's been bad lately."

Erylin grunted. He was more honest than the engineer. A navigator was of use only while he could navigate.

"You know what's happened?" He grunted again as Dumarest nodded. "You saw nothing? No, I thought not. They must have switched to Middle. I've checked the medical kit and drugs are missing."

"I know." Dumarest met the captain's glare. "I took them."

"All of them?"

"Some pain killers. Something to help me get to sleep."

"And I was in the control room. Which leaves you, Fatshan."

"I saw nothing," said the engineer. "Nothing at all."

"Which means they must have left the ship from an

upper port. Well, to hell with it. They're gone. The thing now is what are we going to do about it?" Erylin looked at them, waiting. "Well?"

"A cyber and his acolyte," said Fatshan slowly. "The Cyclan won't like it."

"That helps a lot," sneered the captain. "Chagney?"

"If we report it they'll hold us for questioning. They'll take the ship apart and us with it. They'll never believe we had nothing to do with those men vanishing. I can't believe it myself."

"So?"

Dumarest shrugged. "You're the boss, Captain. But if it was me I'd just keep quiet about it."

"Say nothing?" Fatshan scrubbed at his scalp. "Can we get away with it?"

"We don't know what happened so there's nothing we can tell anyone. We could even be blamed. We certainly aren't going to get paid. A long, wasted journey with nothing but trouble at the end of it. What trader in his right mind wants that?" Dumarest glanced from one to the other knowing he had won. But the decision had to be the captain's. He added, "I'm only making a suggestion, but there's something else to think of. We're carrying cargo. If we hope to stay in business we'd better deliver it. Later, if you want, we can report what's happened."

"The cargo!" Erylin snapped his fingers, relieved at having found the excuse he needed. "That's right. We have a duty to the shippers. We can't be blamed for fulfilling our contract but we'll be taken for pirates if we don't. We'll have to alter course back to Zakym."

And a load would be waiting for transport to another world and from there another and then still more. He would never report the disappearances and neither would the engineer. Even if questioned they could only say that three men had vanished into space and it was doubtful if they would ever be found.

Dumarest felt his knees sag and he stumbled and almost fell against the table. His wound had begun to burn and throb, a wound he would have to disguise until the end. But, to do it, he needed help. Erylin frowned as, straightening, he made his way to the store and drew out a bottle.

101

"Keep a clear head," he snapped. "I want you to plot the course-correction."

The computer would help and the change must be simple. The captain could handle it and Dumarest knew enough about the workings of ships to make a good pretense. Drink and pain, drugs and the ravages of disease would account for the errors he would make.

Now he had something to celebrate.

Lifting the bottle he jerked free the cork and filled his mouth with brandy. He felt the burn of neat spirit against his mouth, the fire which spread down his throat to catch at his lungs and, within seconds, doubled in a paroxysm which tore at his lungs.

"You're mad," said Erylin coldly when Dumarest finally straightened from the bout of coughing. "You can't take that kind of punishment."

"I need it."

"The brandy? You fool! It will kill you!"

"I know." Dumarest looked at the ravaged face reflected in the curved glass. "I know."

Chapter TEN

~~~~~~~~~~~~~~~~~~~~~~~~~~~~~~~~~~~~

The wind that morning was from the north, a strong, refreshing breeze which caught at the mane of her hair and lifted it, sending it streaming like an ebon flag barred with silver. A proud sight, thought Roland as he watched her ride from the courtyard. Proud and stubborn and more than a little willful. Any other would long ago have made her choice, uniting the Family with another, extending the joint holdings and content to do little else but breed children.

Perhaps, if she had been less unusual, he would have been a happier man.

Beyond the gate the road ran straight and clear, a line which ran towards the town to the south and Ellman's Rest to the north. She headed into the wind, revelling in the blast of it against her face, the tug of it at her hair. The day had broken well but the suns were merging in the sky and, when she came in sight of the mound of shattered stone surmounted by the gnarled and twisted tree, she was not surprised to see a figure standing at its foot, another swinging from the topmost branches.

He had died when she'd been a child and had seen him on a morning ride. Her nurse had hurried her away and, later, she had listened to the gossip and learned the story. A herdsman, obviously insane, had taken his life with the aid of a belt looped around his throat. A thwarted lover, so the gossips whispered, who had stolen so as to buy what was denied. Caught, he had escaped before due punishment could be administered and, trapped by approaching darkness, had ended his existence.

It could have been the truth—now she could find out.

Agius Keturlan smiled at her as she dismounted. His face was as wrinkled as ever, as sere as it had been when he had died, but his eyes twinkled as they had done when he had carried her whooping on his shoulders.

"Lavinia, my dear. You are looking well."

"And you, Agius." Her eyes lifted to the swinging shape. "Better than he does."

"An unfortunate."

"A coward."

Gently he shook his head. "Don't be too harsh, my dear. Not all of us can be as strong as you are. How can we tell what torments assailed him? Have you never yearned for love?"

Her blush was answer enough and she turned to adjust her saddle, unwilling to betray more. When she turned again the dangling figure was gone, only the sough of wind stirring the branches.

Only Keturlan remained and she wondered why Charles had not appeared. Why, when she needed him, he remained absent.

The old man said, abruptly, "You are worried, Lavinia. Don't trouble to deny it. It is in your face, the way you stand, the way you walk. Are things not going well?" He grew solemn as she told him of her fears. "Gydapen is a good man in many respects. You could do worse."

"But to be forced?"

"Can any of us be truly free?" His hand lifted before she could answer, a finger pointing towards the swaying branches. "Was that poor fool free? Did he have a choice? Or was he nothing more than the victim of circumstance? We shall never know. But some things we have learned and among them is the realization that not always can we dictate the path we must follow. Can your mount decide? Does it tug, at times, at the rein? Is it a coward because it obeys?"

"Then you advise me to marry Gydapen?"

He smiled and made no answer and, irritated, she looked away towards the loom of the Iron Mountains. Charles would have given her an answer. He would have laughed and joked and made light of the whole thing and she would have been eased and free of the necessity of making a choice.

Was that why he hadn't come?

The animal snorted and pawed the dirt and, after she had soothed it, the old man had gone.

Glancing at the sky she decided against continuing the ride. The day was against it, better to stay at home and settle outstanding details or, better still, to go into town. There could be fresh news of the ship if nothing else. It was overdue —surely now it must arrive soon?

Roland came towards her as she dismounted. His face was anxious.

"Lavinia! Is anything wrong?"

"No. I decided against riding."

"I'm glad." His relief was obvious. "You ride too much alone."

"There is nothing to fear."

"Perhaps." He knew better than to remind her of past escapes. "But the day is against it."

As it was against everything. Shadowy figures stood in secluded corners, vanishing as if made of smoke when approached; old retainers of little interest to any other than their kindred. The place was full of them, men and women who had worked and served and died and were now nothing but vague memories.

Irritably Lavinia shook her head. A hot bath would help and it would follow her usual custom to wash away the grime of riding, but now it was a duty and not a pleasure. But, as she dried herself, welcome news came.

"The ship? At last?"

"It landed a short while ago, my lady." The maid was pleased to deliver the information. "The agent reported your cargo among its load." Her reserve broke a little, familiarity verging on contempt for ancient traditions. "Will there

105

be new gowns? New gems? French perfumes? My lady, if—"

"Enough!"

"My lady!" The girl's eyes lowered in respect, but she could not be blamed. New garments meant the old ones discarded and, for her, a chance to wear expensive finery. "My lady?"

It would be cruel to keep her in suspense.

"I didn't order new gowns," said Lavinia mildly. "Instead there will be a variety of fabrics together with a host of patterns. We shall make our own gowns in the future, and in time, develop our own fashions."

A new industry, perhaps, and certainly a new interest, but if she had expected the girl to display pleasure at the news she was disappointed.

Later Roland explained why.

"She hoped for gifts and you offered her work instead. Why should she be pleased?"

"Why not? I'm giving her the opportunity to create."

"To work," he insisted. "That is the way she regards it. She has no interest in sewing endless stitches or sealing endless seams. It may be a creative enterprise to you but to her, and those who will have to produce the finished product, it is work. You disappointed her. She wanted the result without the effort."

"Laziness!"

"No, Lavinia, a natural desire to obtain the greatest reward for the smallest effort. Some call it the basis of all invention."

"Perhaps." The subject was of no importance and less interest. "When did you think to collect our delivery?"

"Tomorrow." He glanced at the sky. "We could make it before dark but then would have to stay the night. Or we could visit Khaya Taiyuah and move on at dawn." He smiled at the quick, negative jerk of her head. "No?"

"I've no desire to be bored to death. Either Khaya talks about worms or he doesn't talk at all."

"He could have news."

"Of Gydapen? I doubt it. Suspicions, yes, but we have gone into that. The Council made its position clear."

And, at the same time, had shown her her own. A night she remembered as she did the helpless feeling of frustrated rage during which she had bitten her pillow until her teeth had ripped the fabric to shreds.

But Gydapen had since been strangely quiet. He hadn't called as she'd expected and as a persistent suitor would have done. There had been little news as to his activities. For a while she and the other members of the Council had remained tense and poised as if to ward off an expected blow. None had come and the tension had eased a little.

Alcorus, she knew, thought they had called Gydapen's bluff. Navolok that they had met and defeated his challenge. But neither could really conceive of the Pact ever being broken.

And, she thought, neither really could she.

It had been a fact too long. An integral part of the way of life on Zakym. As concrete as the twin suns which hung in the sky. As real as her flesh and blood and bone. They too were a part of this world.

Yet, they too could be broken.

As she, too, could die.

As that man she had seen swinging in the tree at Ellman's Rest. As Charles had died and Keturlan and so many others she had known. All passing on to wait on the far side of the barrier. To return during the periods of delusia. To talk. To warn. To advise.

But, in the end, it was the living who had to make the decisions.

"Tomorrow," she said. "We'll pick up the delivery tomorrow."

But Howich Suchong arrived as they were about to leave with news of odd rumors coming from Gydapen's estate.

Like Taiyuah he was old, like him suspicious, but he had no all-consuming interest in the breeding of new strains cultivating, instead, a wide circle of friendly informants.

"It's odd," he said when, seated in a cool chamber, wine and small cakes set before him, he finally mentioned what had worried him. "You know Gydapen's lands? The arid region to the west?"

"Scrub and sand and little else. Some beasts graze there and there are predators."

Suchong nodded, "But no villages, no arable land, no real

107

reason why a hundred men should have been set to work building hutments."

"No," admitted Roland. "Hutments, you say?"

"Yes."

"A work camp, perhaps?" Lavinia glanced from one to the other. "Something to do with his proposed mining operations?"

"That is what worried me." Suchong took a cake, ate it, wiped crumbs from his lips and delicately sipped at his wine. "The area is beyond that granted by the Sungari. I'd hoped that Gydapen had thought better of his madness but the facts seem to be against it."

"Facts?" She shook her head. "What facts, Howich? Some men building a few shelters—what of it? They could be preparing for a hunt or for herdsmen to take up residence to guard the beasts. I think you worry too much."

"Perhaps." He sipped again at his wine. "But what of the other men who drill at the edge of the desert? And what of the cargo the ship brought here consigned to him?"

"I too have a delivery of goods."

"Most of us had something," he admitted. "But what use could Gydapen have for so much? Large crates and heavy—I saw them when I collected my goods yesterday."

Roland said, "Mining machinery?"

"It could be."

"But you have no proof," said Lavinia. "Only suspicions."

"That is so." Suchong set down his goblet. "But it occurred to me that Gydapen might have said something to you. Confided in you, perhaps?"

"And if he had?"

Suchong sat, his face impassive, an idol carved from weathered stone.

"He has said nothing." Her voice rose a little as he made no comment. "I haven't seen him since the meeting."

He didn't believe her, she knew it, and the knowledge warmed the anger she already felt at his assumption that she would act the spy.

As the silence dragged Roland said, "If Gydapen has been busy as you claim, Howich, he would have had little time for social graces. And he was never a regular visitor here as you know."

"But things have changed since the meeting, surely?"

It was her turn to gain a victory. "Have they, Howich Suchong? Courtesies were exchanged, that is true, and a meal shared—small evidence on which to build vast assumptions. I think that, perhaps, you concern yourself too deeply in the affairs of others."

"Should I sit and ignore my neighbor when his house burns?" His smile was enigmatic. "But, as you have no great loyalty towards Gydapen, you can hardly object to doing a curious old man a favor." His hand fluttered towards his breast. "I have a burning desire for information—an affliction which troubles me at times. But how can I ease it? I have no reason to visit Gydapen but he would not think it strange if you were to call. A long flight to examine your holdings. Some time spent with Taiyuah and then a leisurely journey over the barren lands and the desert to the west. An invitation extended for him to call, perhaps, who could refuse such a charming suppliant?"

"You ask too much, I think!"

"To save the Pact I would demand more!"

Anger flared between them like a sudden fire; his born of determination, hers of the reluctance to play a part and to act the harlot. Then, like a fire which burns too quickly, it died from lack of fuel.

Roland cooled the ashes.

"We will do it," he said. "Lavinia, you can't refuse. Howich, you are not to make a habit of this. But, as you say, the Pact must not be broken."

"The cargo?" It was her last defense, one shattered as he shrugged.

"It can wait."

Wait as they wasted time in tedious conversation and suffered a strained politeness from Khaya Taiyuah. Wait as they moved on, searching, examining, to be met by Gydapen himself when they reached his castle, to be entertained after his fashion. It was more than a week before they returned and she could attend to the cargo the ship had brought.

To open the crates and to find in one of them the limp, apparently dead body of a man.

Chapter ELEVEN

Chagney had taken too long to die. Sitting in a sheltered corner on a high, battlemented promenade, Dumarest recalled how the body, though wasted with disease, had continued stubbornly to function. His own, innate determination to survive had worked against his own interest, adding strength, the power of will. And it had not only been his own.

Warmed by the suns he stared bleakly at a lichened wall remembering how, with the *Sleethan* on its way scant hours after landing on Zakym, he had made an end.

Drugs and alcohol were taking too long and, should it be examined, the wound on his thigh could arouse question. Space was big and empty and clean. A port, cycled, would hurl his body into the void leaving another mystery to add to the rest. Another strange disappearance.

But it had not been easy to do and, as he'd reached for the final lever, there had been a crying deep within his brain.

A crying.

Dumarest felt the constriction of his stomach as he thought about it. It had been real, an intelligence fighting for life, somehow knowing and therefore, somehow aware. Chagney, trapped, helpless, his body usurped, crying at the approach of death.

It had come with air gusting from ruptured lungs, eyes freezing into gelid liquids, the blood fuming in the veins at the sudden release of pressure. For a long, aching moment he had hung naked in the void, shrinking at the vast immensity of the universe, overwhelmed by its tremendous majesty and then had come dissolution.

"Earl!" Lavinia came towards him, striding with a mobile grace along the promenade. She was smiling and the delicate contours of her face held a glowing radiance. "You are awake. Good. I thought you might be asleep."

"I've slept enough."

"Good." She sat beside him and he caught the scent of her perfume. "How do you feel?" She laughed before he could answer. "A stupid question. Why do we ask such things? You almost died—how else would you feel but weak and ill?"

"Grateful."

"For life?"

"For that and for the good luck which gave it to me." Dumarest rose and stretched then took his place again on the bench. "And I am not ill."

"But a little weak?" Concern darkened her eyes. "Too weak to talk?"

"No."

"I am not distressing you?"

"No."

"I am glad of that. Roland thought you would die. I thought you had died. You were so still, so chill, you didn't even seem to be breathing. I couldn't even feel a pulse when you were taken from the crate."

"I was under quick-time," said Dumarest.

"Yes, so Roland explained. He knows about these things. He has travelled while I have not. Yet, even when he'd injected the neutralizer, you still didn't recover. You seemed to be in a coma. It lasted for—well, a long time. And then, when you finally woke, you called my name. At least I thought you did. But it wasn't mine, was it? How could it have been?"

A face which swam from shadows to form shape and substance before his newly opened eyes. One set against a background which accentuated the ebon sheen of the hair, the hauntingly familiar contours of the face. One he had last seen lying in the empty stillness of death.

Lallia!

Long gone now, long dead, as so many other were dead. Ghosts which came to him at times in dreams. Loves which had promised so much.

"Earl!" He felt the touch of her hand against his own, the warm comfort of her fingers. Her eyes met his own, deep, wide with concern. "Is something wrong. Your face—"

"It's nothing."

"So hard," she whispered. "So hurt. So dreadfully bleak."

A face the like of which she had never seen before; one belonging to a man from whom the softness had been burned by the fires of necessity. A man who walked alone. One who knew, as she had never known, the ache of loss, the pain of loneliness.

One who was searching—for what?

"Earth?" she frowned as he answered the question. "An odd name for a world. I've never heard of it. But if you left it surely you can find it again?"

"It was a long time ago," he explained. "I was a boy, ignorant, desperate to escape. I stowed away on a ship. The captain was kind; instead of evicting me as was his right he allowed me to work my passage. I stayed with him until he died."

Moving, always moving towards the center of the galaxy where worlds were close and ships plentiful. Into regions where the very name of Earth was nothing but legend.

"But the coordinates? If you had them a ship could take you back."

"If I had them," he admitted. "But the planet isn't listed in any almanac. No captain admits to ever having heard of the place." He sat, thinking of the long, tiresome search, the determination to discover what he knew must exist. "But I'll find it."

"You seem confident."

"I am." He told her why then ended, dryly, "All I need now is money."

112

A lot of money. A fortune, but that could come later. For now it was enough to sit and feel the warmth of the sunlight, to breath the gentle air and to feel the pulse and surge of life in blood and body. A rustling came from above and a raft glided from the east to hover before settling down into the courtyard.

Idly Dumarest watched it, recognizing the man behind the driver. Lord Roland Acrae who, within minutes, came hurrying along the promenade.

"Lavinia! I must talk with you. Suchong has fresh news and Alcorus—your pardon, Earl. You must excuse me. Are you well?"

An empty question from most; from him a genuine expression of concern.

"Thank you, my lord, yes."

He waved aside the formality.

"That is well. Now, if you will excuse us? Thank you. Lavinia, this cannot wait. Navolok must be consulted at once and we should think seriously. . . ."

His voice faded as he guided the woman along the promenade. To Dumarest she was of normal height, the top of her head coming level with his eyes, but she was at least half a head taller than her companion. Like all the other people of Zakym Dumarest had seen Roland was small, finely built, with a delicate bone structure and a gentle face. The result of centuries of inbreeding, perhaps, or some mutation becoming a dominant genetic trait. Among the scattered worlds of the galaxy such things were common; odd developments produced by the floods of wild radiation which bathed vast areas of space.

In which case Lavinia was an atavar, a throwback to the time when those who had settled this world were taller than now with a more aggressive disposition. That too, he had noticed; a gentleness of behavior which was unusual. Here, on Zakym, it was as if gentle children had come to play, building themselves castles and houses, dividing lands and forming themselves into protective groups, content to let life slip quietly past as they dreamed of endless delights.

A wrong picture, of course, he had seen too little of the place to form a true judgement, but he doubted if it would be too far from fact. A backward world with little com-

113

merce and so few contacts with other, more aggressive cultures. A society founded on farms and animals and a little mining. One producing selectively bred beasts and herbs, plants and insects. There would be few gems and little precious metal. There would be hardly any industry.

A near-static world on which it would be hard for a traveller to gather a stake. Harder still for a stranger to gain a fortune.

Well, that worry would have to wait. He was alive and that was enough.

Dumarest leaned back, feeling the warmth of the lichened stone against his shoulders. The suns were sinking, their orbs close and he closed his eyes against their glare. From the courtyard came little, muted sounds and even the calls of one to another seemed to come from a vast distance or be muffled by layers of cloth.

Odd how the air seemed so ennervating.

Odd how he had woken to imagine Lallia facing him, stooping a little forward, the mane of her hair a shimmering waterfall over rounded shoulders.

A woman.

The womb of creation.

The natural opposite to the harsh reality of death.

Against the closed lids of his eyes Dumarest saw again the distant burn of scattered stars, the sheets and curtains of luminescence, the somber patches of darkness, the fuzz of remote nebulae—and felt, too, the aching emptiness of the space into which he had flung himself.

To drift in the embracing shimmer of the Erhaft field, to break from it, to hang utterly alone. To die.

To hear the thin, so thin, crying. The crying . . . the crying . . .

"No!" Her jerked awake with a gasp, aware that he had dozed, feeling the wetness of sweat on his face, the tremble of his hands. He had killed before and had seen men die and had heard them plead before they died but never had it been like this.

The crying. The thin, plaintive, hopeless crying.

"It doesn't matter, Earl." The voice was a familiar wheeze. "It doesn't matter at all."

Chagney!

He stood with his back against the stone wall of the battlement, dressed as Dumarest had remembered, his face the same, the eyes clear, the mouth free of the frill of blood which it must have worn at the last. Now, standing, he smiled and extended a hand.

"We all have to go, Earl. Sooner or later it comes to us all. And what did I lose? A few days? A week? Zakym would have been my last planetfall."

A dead man standing, talking, smiling, his eyes clear—but how?

"Does it matter?" Thin shoulders lifted in a shrug as Chagney turned to look over the crenellated wall. "You have died, Earl. You know more than most. You died—and I died with you!"

Chagney!" Dumarest stepped forward, reaching, feeling stone. He leaned against it for a moment, feeling tension at the base of his skull. The dominant half of the affinity twin had nestled there—could it still, in some incredible manner, be connected with the part Chagney had carried?

Would death never end?

Dumarest drew in his breath and straightened. The promenade was empty, the navigator had vanished, but some of the tension remained. Theoretically the affinity twin should dissolve when the bond was broken, the basic elements being absorbed into the metabolism, but what if theory was wrong?

"Earl!" Kalin smiled, her hair a rippling flame. "Think of it as a transceiver. You are never really in the host-body at all. It is just that all sensory data is transmitted and received on the ultimate level of efficiency. The rest is illusion."

Kalin? Here?

She vanished as he took a step towards her and he stumbled and fell to a knee, hands outstretched, feeling the rasp of stone on his palms, a growing madness.

The promenade, once empty, was now thronged with figures. Men, women, some strange, others vaguely familiar, a few seeming to gain solidity as he watched. The man he had fought on Harald, falling with blood on his lips, eyes glazed in hatred as he died. The gentle face of Armand Ramhed, the ruined one of his assassin, the sly eyes of an old woman from . . . from . . . and then, shockingly, he was looking at himself.

A man lying pale and limp and apparently dead. A man who dissolved and rose and stood tall and menacing in a scarlet robe.

Cyber Broge, his face like a skull, bone which smiled.

"There's no escape, Dumarest. We are too powerful. You can never hope to elude us for long. We shall find you and, when we do, you will pay." The even tones echoed as if rolling down a corridor. "Pay . . . pay . . . pay . . ."

His arm lifted and Dumarest sprang to one side, hand dropping to his boot, the hilt of the knife carried there, rising with it gleaming naked in his hand, lunging forward to send the steel whining through the air in a vicious cut which drew sparks from stone, ripped at fabric—and sent Roland Acrae falling back with a rip on the sleeve of his blouse.

"Earl! No!" Lavinia came running towards him as again the blade rose. It halted in its driving lunge to fall inches from the ruined blouse, light turning the steel into a purple shimmer, luminescent blurs riding the honed edge and point.

"A mistake." Dumarest lowered the knife. "I thought—it was a mistake. I apologize, my lord."

"So fast." Roland lifted fingers to the ripped sleeve. "You moved like the wind."

"A mistake."

"The mistake was mine." Incredibly he was calm. "I should have known, have warned you, at least. "Look at the suns."

They were very close, edges almost touching, flares of magenta and violet filling the air with a purple haze.

"I could have killed you," said Dumarest. And would have done if something, instinct perhaps, had not stayed his hand. Lavinia added to the strangeness of the moment with her smile.

"You could have done, I suppose, and if you had I would have regretted it. But it would not have been the tragedy you seem to think."

"My lady?"

"He would have moved on but he wouldn't have wholly

gone. At times of delusia he would have returned. We could have spoken to him and he to us."

"Delusia?" Dumarest looked again at the suns beginning to understand. "Is that when the dead come back to life?"

"We can see them and talk to them and they to us. Is that what disturbed you? The presence of an old enemy who threatened you? One who wanted to hurt?"

"One who wanted to kill."

"And so you tried to kill him." Slowly she nodded, her eyes wide, the lift of her breasts prominent beneath her gown as she drew in her breath. "Do you find it easy to kill, Earl?"

He thought of Chagney. "No."

"But, if you are threatened, you will?"

"It is the way of life." Dumarest looked at the knife and thrust it back into his boot. "You breed animals and must know that. The strongest are those who perpetuate their line. To do that they will fight and win. They have to win."

"Animals are not men."

"Perhaps not, my lady, but the same rule applies. A man is nothing if he is not alive—dead he can only feed the ground."

"On Zakym men do not truly die," said Lavinia swiftly. "No human dies. They are changed. Delusia is proof of that."

"Proof?"

"You have seen it, Earl. You know."

He said, dryly, "You believe the dead return to confer with you. That, at certain times, you break some barrier or that some barrier is broken. But always those you see are those you remember. Always, am I right?"

"Yes, but—what has that to do with it? They are real. They talk and smile and listen. You have seen them for yourself. That man you tried to kill—proof, Earl! Proof!"

He heard the conviction in her voice, saw it in her eyes, the stance of her body. To argue against faith was to try and blow out a sun. The evidence was there, to her beyond question, a comfort she could not reject.

"Earl?"

"My lady, I am a stranger to this world, alive only be-

117

cause of your hospitality. Who am I to question your ways?"

"But—"

"Lavinia!" Roland rested his hand on her arm. "You upset yourself without cause. Not all worlds know what we know. Delusia is unique to Zakym. It takes time to understand."

The man had travelled and would know more than he said. Dumarest glanced at the sky, at the twin suns with their tremendous energy-potential, solar furnaces blasting radiation into space. A flood which was subtly altered when the suns merged to become a pattern of forces which distorted the micro-currents of the brain and so create hallucinations. Fragments of memory, revived, projected, given attributes which existed only in the minds of the beholder.

Delusions which would form the basis of a religion, a faith, a way of life.

"Earl?" Lavinia took a step towards him, her eyes searching his face. "You understand?"

A person who communed with the dead. A tall and lovely woman whose hair glowed with the lambent sheen of purple light from the setting suns. One who flushed a little as she felt her body respond to his masculinity.

Roland, watching, said abruptly, "It's getting late. We had best go below."

Chapter TWELVE

The room was similar to others he had known; the walls of stone softened with hanging fabrics, the floor of polished wood, the bed soft and the covers delicately embroidered with a variety of hues anl patterns. Dumarest lifted one and let it run through his fingers. It held an engaging primitiveness and, on more sophisticated worlds, would have commanded a high price.

Letting it fall Dumarest crossed to the window. It was small, fitted with hexagonal panes, looking on to a shaft faced with white stone. Reflected light from one side and above revealed another chamber, more lay to the sides and lower down. No window faced another. The panes, locked in their frame, were impossible to open.

A knock, and a servant entered bearing a lighted lamp. Setting it on a small table the girl curtsied.

"My lord, your bath is ready and soon it will be curfew."

"Thank you." Dumarest had heard the throb of the gong before. "Does it always sound at night?"

"At dark, yes, my lord. The castle is sealed then."

"Totally?" He smiled at her blank expression. "If I wanted to go out could I?"

119

"Out, my lord?" the concept was beyond her comprehension. "Go out? But why?"

"To take a walk, maybe. Could I? Is there a gate?"

"No." She shuddered a little. "Not open, my lord. But it would be madness to go out after dark. Madness!"

"Why?"

"The—my lord, you must excuse me. I have duties to attend to. Things to be done before curfew."

He gestured dismissal and returned to the window. Leaning against the panes he stared up at the sky. Only a little was visible, a deep indigo in which shone fitful gleams, the patch edged with a rim of stone. As he watched shapes appeared; men who lifted something to let it fall and block the opening. A seal of some kind which shut out the world beyond.

The throb of the gong came as he entered the bath. It thrummed through the building, creating tintinnabulations on all sides so that the very air quivered to the solemn beat.

Dumarest ducked his head, felt the vibration through the water and rose to see Roland standing beside the tub. He handed Dumarest a towel, watched with envious eyes as he dried himself, the fabric rasping over the firm muscles of shoulders and back, the lean lines of hips and waist.

Without preamble he said, "On the promenade, when you tried to kill me, what did you see?"

"An enemy."

"And you struck out like that? Without thought or hesitation?"

"Should I have waited for him to kill me first?"

"Perhaps not." Roland found a chair and sat, thoughtful. "As you may have noticed, Earl, we are a peaceful race. The thought of violence is strange to us. We live now as we have lived for centuries—in common harmony. There are minor frictions, of course, we are individuals and that is inevitable, but the turning to violence which is so common on other worlds is not in our nature. You—" He broke off, looking at his hands. "You are a stranger among us—do you understand what I am trying to say?"

"Tell me."

"Lavinia is a very beautiful woman as you must have noticed. She is, however, on the edge of marrying one of our number."

"You?"

"The Lord Gydapen Prabang. He has a great influence and the marriage must take place if certain unpleasant effects are to be avoided. You are an intelligent man, Earl. You must have noticed how attracted Lavinia is to you. I can understand that. Against the rest of us you are—unusual. But you have no roots here, no responsibilities. Perhaps you consider you are in debt towards us?"

Dumarest nodded, saying nothing.

"It is something I regret having to mention but I am left with little choice. You could, if you wished, cause great damage. Lavinia—"

"Is a woman old enough to make up her own mind."

"True, but, against your experience, she is little more than a child. I saw your expression when on the promenade. You said nothing but I knew what you were thinking. Lavinia believes in delusia, you do not. Think of the gap which that alone forms between you. And there are others."

As he paused Dumarest said, knowing the answer, "What do you want me to do?"

"Be cold. Turn her away from you. Save her marriage and, at the same time, save this world."

"Is the marriage as important as that?"

"Yes." Roland shook his head as he saw Dumarest's incredulity. "You cannot understand, but take my word for it, please. If you accept that you are in debt then settle it this way. Do as I ask."

And if he refused? On other worlds the answer would have been direct; a stab in the back, an assassin hired, poison slipped into food or wine. Death or maiming delivered with merciless precision. Great Families knew how to take care of their own.

But here?

The fact that Roland was pleading was answer enough. Proof of his fear and proof of more than he realized.

Dumarest said, evenly, "I am a traveller. If I had money enough I would take passage on the first ship to leave."

"That can be arranged!" The man's relief was obvious. "Money can be found!"

"Then we are agreed?"

"Yes, Earl, we are agreed." Roland stepped towards the door. "Dinner will be in thirty minutes. A servant will guide you when you are ready."

It was a long and leisurely affair; dishes rich in protein served in a variety of ways; little morsels of meat wrapped in leaves, fruits, dusted with crushed nuts, dipped in astringent sauces, charred in flame, steeped in compotes of a dozen kinds. Salvers held items of pastry, blends of creams and pastes, miniature figures of succulent crispness, oozing semi-liquid delights. There were wines; some tart and refreshing which cleansed the palate, others warm and tantalizing, chilled and spiced, tasting of fruit and bitter roots. One holding within its purple depths the taste of effulgent bubbles.

"We make it only once each year," Lavinia explained. "From pods delivered to us in exchange for various other items. It is brewed in ancient caskets to an old recipe and sealed in bottles of black glass. A little lifts the spirit but more will open doors and give you glimpses of the unknown which you may regret. It is wise to be moderate."

"In all things." Dumarest had barely touched the variety of dishes, eating only from those selected by Roland. The man could be genuine—but to take precautions would do no harm.

"Yes, Earl, in all things." Lavinia clapped her hands. "In love, in life and in entertainment."

Music rose from a shadowed alcove where a small group sat with their instruments. The throb of drums merged with the thin, high wailing of pipes, the steady thrumming of plucked strings. It softened into a steady beat as an old man stepped forward to chant an involved saga dealing with an incredible journey through tremendous perils with final success. He bowed as coins showered at his feet to be followed by a troupe of young girls who danced with agile abandon.

Lavinia watched them, glancing at Dumarest, noting his attention. Beneath her fingers a morsel of bread crumbled to an untidy litter of crumbs.

"You like them, Earl?"

"They seem accomplished."

"You would like one? The one with the big mouth, for example? Or the one with the blonde hair?"

"Are they yours to give, my lady?"

"I—"

"Are they slaves?"

"There are no slaves on Zakym." Roland leaned forward, quick to soothe, aware of tension. "Lavinia was joking, Earl. She is a little jealous, I think."

"Of the dancers?" Dumarest was deliberately obtuse. "They are very skilled and it no doubt takes years of training to achieve such perfection, but, even so, I think you could hold your own with them, my lady."

"It is gracious of you to say so." Her tone was chill. "I, the Mistress of the Family, a common dancer. Well, I suppose there are worse fates. But assuming they were slaves and you desired one and I gave her to you, what then?"

"I would set her free."

"As a reward for pleasing you?"

Dumarest said, flatly, "Have you ever been a slave, my lady? Have you ever felt the weight of the collar of servitude? To know that disobedience means torment and could mean your life? No. Of course you haven't. If you had you would never talk so lightly of slaves. They are people, not things. Men and women with feelings, not items to be bought and used and sold."

"Earl. Lavinia was joking."

Dumarest looked at the hand Roland had rested on his arm. A small hand, the fingers thin, delicate, like the limbs of a spider—no, like the helpless appendages of a child. But a gesture from them could rob him of freedom. He was alone in a sealed castle, one against the servants and retainers, trapped in a place from which there could be no escape.

It was a time to be cautious.

"You spoke with feeling, Earl." Lavinia lifted a hand to the column of her throat as if feeling for the metal caress of a collar. "You have a hatred of those who would make slaves of others."

"Yes, my lady."

"Because you have worn the collar yourself, perhaps?" She gave him no time to answer. "No matter. If you have it is no doubt an experience you never wish to repeat. So many experiences, Earl. You must tell me more about them later."

"As you wish, my lady." Dumarest felt the impact of Roland's eyes. "But would it be wise?"

"What do you mean?"

"I understood that you were betrothed. Wouldn't your future husband object?"

"Gydapen? The Lord of Prabang?" Her laugh was brittle. "Who cares about him?"

"I do, my lady. He could be jealous and none could blame him for that. He has influence on this world and I have none. It would be best for me to take a room in a hotel in town. Then when a ship arrives, I can arrange passage."

"No!" Her rejection was too sharp and she realized it, making an effort to control her tone before she spoke again. "That is unnecessary, Earl. You are a welcome guest. Tell him so, Roland. Tell him he is welcome. What must I do in order to persuade him to stay?"

"Lavinia, Earl is being wise."

"No!"

"It is best that he should go. Here there could be danger and we must not expose him to unnecessary risks. He—"

"Roland, you talk like a fool!" She was impatient, taking his words at their face value, not realizing their true intent. Gentle at heart she would never force another to remain at risk. "What danger could threaten Earl? Who would dare to challenge him? He is no stranger to violence but here we are a peaceful people. We—"

"Peaceful?" Dumarest was curt in his interruption. The thing had been decided—it was time to end the useless argument. "I think you are mistaken, my lady. If they are so peaceful then why are they importing guns?"

"Guns?" Roland was incredulous. "Earl, are you sure?"

"How can he be sure?" Lavinia was equally as disbelieving. "How?"

"I've seen them." Dumarest looked from one to the other, remembering the story he had told to account for his being in the crate. "I was stranded on Harald as I've told you. I broke into a warehouse intending to hide in some cargo and so gain passage to another world. To become a stowaway. I had to be careful, the penalty if discovered is eviction."

"And?"

"I checked the crates. One of them was filled with guns. I resealed the crate and opened another—and the rest you know."

"Were the crates bound for Zakym?" Roland pressed the point. "Were they?"

"Yes."

"Was it marked in any way? The crate holding the guns, I mean?"

"A symbol," said Dumarest, slowly. "The sign of an axe crossed with a scythe."

"The whole enclosed in a circle?" Roland glanced at the woman as Dumarest nodded. "Gydapen's mark."

"Gydapen." Her finger traced a random pattern in the litter of crumbs. "But what use would he have for guns? Mining machinery, yes, that would be expected, but guns? Why guns?"

"They are usually needed in order to fight a war," said Dumarest, dryly. "But wouldn't you know about his intentions? As his proposed wife wouldn't he have confided in you?"

"They all ask that," she snapped. "The answer is no. The marriage, if ever it takes place, will be a political one. I know nothing about his guns, his sheds, his men out marching. Nothing about his ambitions. Only his threats."

"Sheds?" Dumarest glanced at Roland, listened as he explained. The journey over the wastelands, what had been spotted from the raft. "Long sheds like extended huts?"

"Yes."

"And were the men marching in line or column? Did they act oddly at times—all moving in unison for example? Were others standing to one side?"

Roland nodded and said, "You suspect something, Earl. What?"

"In my experience guns and sheds and marching men usually add up to one thing. Someone is training a group of men to follow orders. The sheds are to house them and the guns are to arm them when they are ready to fight."

"To fight?" Lavinia looked from one to the other. "To kill, you mean? No! It's unthinkable. You must have made a mistake. Not even Gydapen could get his men to kill others."

"You would be surprised at what men can be persuaded to do," said Dumarest, dryly. "And it takes little to point a weapon and pull the trigger. To many it isn't killing at all. It is just a sport and their victims moving targets. After the first time it comes easy. The more so if a bonus is paid to every good shot."

"It's disgusting!"

"Yes, but it happens."

Roland said, "I was talking to the agent. Gydapen had a score of crates delivered. If they all contained guns he would have enough to arm every man on his estates. But why?" He found an answer as he voiced the question. "To stop us preventing his mining operation. He's determined to break the Pact no matter what the Council may decide. The others must be warned—but how to stop him? What to do?"

"You have guns," said Dumarest. "Enforce your will."

"Demand that he obeys?" Roland shook his head. "Our arms are limited. We have a few lasers, some hunting rifles and little else. We depend on moral persuasion. Against Gydapen it will not be enough."

"Then steal his weapons. A night attack would catch him by surprise. The guns are still probably in their crates. They could be found, used if necessary. Darkness would cover the operation."

"No, Earl. Not at night. That would be impossible."

"But it would give you the best chance." Dumarest glanced at the woman and saw her determined expression. "No?"

"No, Earl. As Roland says it is impossible."

"But why? If—" Dumarest broke off and shrugged. "Well, it's none of my concern. Tomorrow I leave for the town."

"Earl!"

"He intends to leave," said Roland. "We had come to an understanding. I would like to cancel it, Earl, if I may. Instead I would like to offer another. Help us and I guarantee you the price of a dozen High passages. More if possible."

Money to buy passage, to pay for computer time, cash to open the door to the whereabouts of Earth. And to earn it?

"We need peace," said Roland. "We need to borrow your strength. Gydapen must be stopped. Unless he is—" his voice broke, recovered with an effort. "Those guns—the Pact—who can help us if you will not?"

Chapter
THIRTEEN

A spider had cast its web in one corner of the room, that or some ancient tremor had cracked the plaster into the resemblance of lace and, lying on the soft comfort of the wide bed, Dumarest studied it through half-closed eyes. In the flicker of lamplight it took on new and more fantastic configurations; the shape of an engine, a face, a pair of intermeshed hands. The blur of a spectrogram, the straggle of a dead man's hair, the pattern of a retina.

A mystic symbol seen by chance and which could hold all the secrets of time.

As the castle held mystery.

It was sealed tight, no means of egress left unbarred, the upper stairs blocked as was the shaft beyond the window. Life, on Zakym, ceased at sunset or, rather, grew introverted with each making his own entertainment, small groups congregating, guests caught by the approach of darkness willingly found accommodation as if the night held dreadful peril.

Another delusion as was the belief in the dead rising to live again?

If it was a delusion.

How could he ever be sure?

Yet there could be no denying Roland's panic at the mention of the guns or of the woman's fear of what they could portend. A fear which added her voice to the man's as, together, they had pleaded for him to stay. To help. To die, perhaps, in their cause.

Suddenly impatient, Dumarest rolled from the bed and rose to his feet. He had lain down fully dressed and now stepped quietly towards the door. Outside the passage was silent in the dull glow of shaded lamps. One end led to a stair which, as he knew, was barred. The other met a descending way. As he reached it, Lavinia appeared from her room.

"Earl? Is that you?"

"It is, my lady."

"This formality!" She made an impatient gesture. "It stifles me. I thought we had settled that. Why are you here? Can't you sleep?"

"No."

"Why not?" Her slippers rustled as she stepped closer towards him. She wore a robe of diaphanous material belted at the waist and her hair, like a gleaming waterfall striped with silver, rippled over the smooth rotundity of her shoulders. The hand she rested on his arm was a sculptor's delight. "Earl?"

"I need to plan but there is too much I don't know. The lie of the land, distances, numbers—have you maps of the area?"

They were in a room redolent of dust and mildew. Thin sheets crackled as they were unrolled, marked with carefully drawn lines, various areas marked in differing colors, small pennants set above miniature castles.

"Here!" The tip of a finger marked a point. "This is where we are. Over here lies the domain of Khaya Taiyuah. This is the estate of Fhard Erason. Here—"

"Gydapen's lands?"

"Suchong's. This is Gydapen's and here are the wastes where the hutments are to be found."

Dumarest studied them. "Water? Is there a stream close to hand?"

"No."

"A well, then? An artesian boring?" He pursed his lips as she shook her head. Men training beneath hot suns needed plenty of water. If it had to be carried then the local air would be busy.

"Did you see the smoke of fires? No. A line of men waiting to be served?"

"How would I know, Earl?"

"If you saw them you would know." He studied the old map again. "This is all high ground, right?"

He frowned as she nodded, tracing the shading, spotting the general lay of the area. It had been chosen with care. From various points lookouts could spot any approach and fast movement towards the place on foot would be difficult.

"When you examined the area did you notice anything different about any of the huts? No? Then have you seen or heard of a stranger being maintained by Gydapen either in his castle or in town?"

"A stranger? No, Earl. How would he have arrived without us knowing?"

"How did I arrive?" Dumarest shugged at her expression. "I may be wrong but I'd gamble there is someone. A man trained in the art of fighting. A mercenary perhaps—you said that your people had a reluctance to fight?"

"That is so."

"Then a teacher would have had to be found. Those who handled the shipping of the guns could have provided him and others might follow."

"An army?"

"Men trained and willing to kill. Men used to the art of war. On some worlds they come cheap. Well, perhaps we can delay them. Tomorrow I'll pick some men. A night attack and—"

"No. We can't attack at night. The Pact forbids it."

"The Pact?"

"The Sungari. Earl, why do you think we are so afraid of what Gydapen may do? If he breaks the Pact it will affect us all. At all costs he must be stopped from doing that. Our very lives depend on it!"

And his own too, presumably, a fallacy in her reasoning

but Dumarest didn't mention it. Instead he said, "The Sungari? Just what and who are they?"

She told him over wine, filling goblets with her own hands, handing him one and sitting to crouch at his feet, lamplight streaming over her shoulders, reflected with a nacreous glow from the half-revealed mounds of her breasts, the curves of her thighs.

"When the first settlers came to Zakym they found the world already occupied by a different form of life. One which was not native to the place and which was willing to share. At first there was trouble but sense prevailed and the Pact was formed."

She paused to sip wine and Dumarest leaned back, filling in gaps, building a whole from the story which she told.

A time of attrition, of fear and battle, of terror even from the things which happened at night. Then the agreement. Men were to have the surface of the world and the Sungari the depths. Men were to rule by day and the Sungari by night. Certain areas of surface and depths were given for the sole use of the other. Herds and crops were to be left untouched. Native game was common to both. The night mist which came to wreath the ground belonged to the Sungari.

Death came to any human foolish enough to be out at night.

Dumarest said, dryly, "How long has it been since such a thing happened?"

"A long time ago, Earl." She turned her head to look up at him, the long line of her throat framed by the mantle of her hair. "But it happened."

"And has anyone ever seen a Sungari?"

"They exist, Earl!"

"Has anyone ever seen them?"

"How could they when they only come out at night?"

"And everyone is snug indoors by then?" Dumarest nodded, wondering why the story had been started. "An easy way to impose authority? The warped design of a twisted mind? All to be safe indoors at night with whispered horrors as a spur to obey. A deliberate conditioning engineered by someone with a terror of the dark?

It was possible. In the universe all things were possible.

131

Many strange cultures had risen from seeds planted by the founders of small colonies governed by freakish convictions. Holphera where men walked backwards for fear of meeting death. Andhara where no woman looked directly at the face of her child but always used a mirror. Inthelle where the old were given all they could desire for a month and then killed and ceremoniously eaten. Chage where each birth had to be accompanied by a death. Xanthis where women ruled and men grovelled at their feet.

"Earl?" Lavinia looked up with luminous eyes. "You are so quiet. Don't you believe me?"

To argue with her was useless. She, all of Zakym, believed in the living presence of the dead—against such conviction what chance had logic?

"Earl?"

"I was thinking." His hand fell to touch the silken strands of her hair. "Unless you are willing to attack at night there is only one other thing to do. Gydapen cannot be a fool. He will have anticipated the possibility of the Council moving against him and will have taken elementary precautions. If we assemble a large force it will be spotted. Therefore we must go in with the minimum number."

"How many?"

"Two." He heard the sharp intake of her breath. "Just you and I in the largest raft you have. We'll pay a visit to the barren wastes."

"And?"

"That depends on what we find." Some wine remained in the goblet and Dumarest drank it before rising to his feet. "You had better get some rest now. Tomorrow you need to look your best."

They left at dawn, rising high and heading towards the west before swinging in a wide circle which would bring them back over Gydapen's land. The raft was a plain, commercial affair, devoid of any decoration aside from a blazon on the prow. The body was open, edged with a solid rail, the controls shielded by a curved, transparent canopy. The engine which fed power to the anti-grav units was too small for the bulk of the vehicle and progress was slow.

From where she sat at his side, Lavinia said, "Earl,

you are a man of many surprises. Where did you learn to handle a raft?"

"I forget."

"And to fight? Where did you learn that?"

On Earth as a boy, a time he would never forget. Life had been hard and devoid of comfort. There had been no toys, no easy times, regular food or loving care. He had hunted vermin with a sling, gutting his prey with a jagged stone, eating the meat raw because a fire would have betrayed his position to those who would have stolen his kill.

"Earl?"

With the insistence of a child she wanted an answer or, bored, merely wanted to talk.

"It doesn't matter."

"It does to me." Her hand reached out to touch his arm and she wondered if he guessed how little she had slept. "I'd like to know all about you. You are so strong, so self-sufficient. Don't you ever get tired of travelling? Have you never been tempted to settle down?"

Too often, yet always something had happened to smash the dream and, always, the yearning was present to find his home.

"At times, yes."

"But you never did? Of course not, it was a stupid question. If you had then you wouldn't be here now."

Her hand closed on his arm, the fingers digging into his flesh, then was snatched away as, abruptly, the raft tilted and fell. An air pocket of lesser density, a momentary hazard quickly overcome and again the raft rose and levelled. Below the terrain became a blur, the ground blotched with hills, rolling scrub, grassy plateaus, the silver thread of a river.

"Taiyuah's boundary," she said. "And there is an emergency stop-over."

It was a low, black building fitted with a single door and holding, as Dumarest had learned, bottles of wine, food, some medical supplies. A haven for those who should be lost or crash nearby.

"You have many of them?"

"Of course. We set them up for common use. People use them if they are caught by night."

"As protection against the Sungari?"

"Yes, Earl. As a defense."

A bolster to the illusion, he thought, as the building passed beneath them far below. Once create a situation and props fell automatically into place. The curfew, tunnels connecting close-set buildings such as were to be found in the town, and in the open ground places which could shut out the darkness.

The raft dropped again, rose, headed slowly on its way. The lift was strong as was to be expected in a transport but that was all. Dumarest glanced at the sky judging the position of the suns. They had passed the zenith and were edging towards the horizon. It had been a long, monotonous flight and the woman was hungry.

"Can we land and eat, Earl?"

"We haven't the time."

"But—"

"Eat as we go. You can handle a raft, of course? Good. We'll take turns at the controls. Keep us high. I want to arrive with the suns behind us."

Two hours later the hutments came into sight.

Dumarest was at the controls and he veered the raft, watching, studying the terrain. The buildings were set in a row, another crossways at the rear, one, larger, placed well to one side. Before them the ground was level, set with swollen bags set on tripods.

"They weren't here before, Earl." Lavinia looked up from her binoculars. "What are they?"

"Water containers. The hut crossways to the others is probably a latrine. The large one could house the man I spoke of."

"The mercenary?"

"If there is one, yes. He'll be using it as living quarters and command office. The range?" Dumarest scanned the terrain as he kept one hand on the controls. In the field of his binoculars the view skittered as the craft hit uneven air. "Look for a firing range of some kind. A flat space ending in a mound. There could be targets."

A moment, then she said, "Nothing like that, Earl. Not that I can see. There are some cairns set well to one side. A row of them."

"Any men?"

"A few. They are facing the cairns. They seem to be holding something."

"Guns." Dumarest lowered the binoculars. "Those heaps of stone are targets. Get ready now. We're going in."

It was madness, a display of naked audacity and yet, as Dumarest had pointed out, Gydapen had no reason to be suspicious beyond the range of normal caution. The arrival of the guns, as far as he knew, was still a secret. Lavinia, aware of his interest in her, intrigued as any woman would be in a similar situation, would naturally pay a visit. And, as a member of the Council, she had every right to inspect the proposed mining installation.

Things he had painstakingly explained during the journey, impatient with her objections.

"A spy!" she'd blurted. "You want me to act the spy. Just like Taiyuah!"

"He was right."

"But—"

"If you know a better way let me hear it. No? Then do as I say."

And now they were slanting down in the glare of the suns to skim over the buildings and come to a landing close beside the larger construction.

The man who came to greet them was a worker from Gydapen's estate but one who had undergone a subtle change. It was manifest in the way he stood, the tilt of his head, the something—a touch of arrogance?—in his eyes.

Yet his voice was gentle and his words polite.

"My lady! How may I serve you?"

"You know who I am?"

"Of course. You are the Lady Lavinia Del Belamosk. A member of the Council—"

"And a close friend of your master. Is he here?" Then, before the man could answer, she snapped, "Never mind. I was to have been met. Well, perhaps he has been delayed. While I'm waiting you will show me around."

She carried herself well, speaking with a curt imperiousness, forcing the man's attention. For a moment he hesitated, then bowed, extending a hand to help her descend from the raft. Dumarest watched as they headed towards

the open space then, dropping over the far side of the
craft, walked without hesitation towards the nearest hut.

As he'd suspected it was fitted as a dormitory, the floor
of tamped dirt, the cots flimsy metal frames bearing thin
mattresses and a single cover. There were no windows.
Each end was pierced by a door. Lamps stood with a clutter
of small items of a personal nature on narrow shelves. A
table stood in the center of the floor ringed with benches.
It carried a heap of plates, a container of water and a dozen
earthenware cups. The air held the unmistakable odor of
too many men living too close.

Nowhere could he see any sign of weapons.

The rear door opened on a narrow space faced with
the hut set crosswise to the others. He had been wrong
about its purpose. Half was a cooking area with fires burning
beneath metal plates on which stood containers of stew.
The other half was locked. The latrine he found by its odor;
poles set over a trench dusted with a chemical compound,
the whole shaded by a camouflaged curtain. It lay well to
one side and, at a thought, Dumarest checked the hut he had
first entered. At the side of the rear door was a couple of
lidded buckets—for use in case of need during the night.

Two men looked at him as he left the hut and moved to
the next. He met their eyes.

"You! Who is in charge of these huts?"

"Sir?" One of them blinked.

"Are you deaf? Didn't you near me? Who is in charge
of these huts? You?"

"No, sir." The man looked at his companion. "Jarl. I'm
his helper."

"Helping him to do what—loaf?" Dumarest made his
tone acid. "The huts are a disgrace. Dirt everywhere. Cots
untidy. The tables unwiped—" He turned, scowling. "Let
me see this one. Take the lead. Move!"

Shaken they obeyed. Dumarest examined the hut, finding
it much like the other, his eyes counting beds as he pre-
tended to find patches of dirt, fluff, drifted sand where no
sand should be. Again there was no sign of weapons.

Leaving the two men inside the hut Dumarest stepped
outside towards the rear, signaled at a small group which

had just left the cookhouse, glared at them as they came to a halt.

"Slovenly. Haven't you been taught elementary drill? Well, haven't you?"

"Sir!" One of the men drew himself to attention.

"Good." Dumarest nodded at the man. "The rest of you fall out. Wait in that hut until I call for you. You—your name? Hoji? Tell me, Hoji, where are the weapons kept?"

A gamble. If the man knew he might unthinkingly give the direction. If he didn't then the question could be covered and no harm would be done.

"The weapons, sir?"

"The guns." Dumarest grunted as the man's eyes flickered to the rear of the cookhouse. "Not moved yet? Why not? Well, never mind. Call those men and have them report to the weapons-store. Move!"

Time gained for him to move to the door and send his knife probing into the lock. It was heavy but basically simple. A click and it was open. As the men returned Dumarest threw wide the door.

Inside rested a heap of crates, some open. On the top of one rested a half-dozen guns together with boxes of ammunition.

"Those!" Dumarest pointed at the crates. "Load them into the raft standing before the huts. Hurry!"

Men accustomed to obey rarely hesitated if orders were given in a tone of authority. A fact Dumarest knew and had relied on. They didn't know who or what he was, but his voice held the snap of command and, to them, it was unthinkable that he should order without having the right.

Dumarest stepped back as the first crate was shifted. A gun fell from the loose pile and he picked it up, looking at the piece. It was cheap, crude, now cleaned of grease and fitted with a full magazine. He cocked it, watched the cartridges spill from the ejector, removed the magazine and, after clearing the breech, pulled the trigger.

As the harsh click faded a voice said, "Well, friend, what do you think of it?"

He was tall, slouched, his mouth scarred so that the upper lip was set in a permanent smile. He wore stained clothing frayed at wrists and collar, the leather bearing shiny patches and marks where badges could have been. His hair was dark, his eyes wells of coldness. In his right hand he held a compact laser.

It hung loose in his fingers, not aimed but the muzzle swinging casually in Dumarest's direction.

Dumarest shugged. "It's cheap. It'll jam. It isn't accurate and it'll pull to the right. But it will do if nothing else is around."

"Such as?"

"That laser you're carrying." Dumarest threw down the weapon he held. "Didn't the boss tell you we were coming?"

"Should he have done?"

"Why ask me? I only work here." Dumarest stepped aside as the men returned for another load, a step which took him closer to the mercenary. "How are things here? Good pay? Lots of fun?"

"Out here? You must be joking."

"Well, at least you can't spend anything. When did you land? Ship before last? The one before that?"

"When did you?" The man scowled as Dumarest gave no answer. "What the hell are you doing here, anyway?"

"Shifting the guns."

"Why? To where?"

Dumarest shrugged, deliberately casual. To browbeat the mercenary would be a mistake. To explain too fully another.

"Don't ask me. I came here with his woman and she gave the orders. I guess she got them from him. Have you ever seen her?"

"No."

"She's outside looking around. It might pay you to remember her. Look between the huts and you could spot her." Dumarest took a step forward, hand lifting as he pointed, another and now he was close to the mercenary, the weapon he held. "There she is! See!"

The jerk of his hand demanded attention. As the man lifted his head, eyes narrowing against the glare it turned, the palm stiffening, slashing down like a blunted axe in a savage chop which would have snapped the wrist like a twig. Instead, at the last moment, Dumarest altered the direction so it glanced over the fingers and sent the laser hurtling to the ground.

"What the hell!" The mercenary swore, rubbing his fingers. "You damned near broke my hand!"

Dumarest said nothing, stepping forward to pick up the weapon, looking down the space between the huts at the woman who strode towards him, the man at her side, the armed guards at his rear.

"Earl," said Lavinia steadily. "This is Lord Gydapen Prabang. Gydapen, meet Earl Dumarest."

She had the sense not to say more.

Chapter
FOURTEEN

"Earl Dumarest." Gydapen lifted his goblet and tilted it so the wine it contained left a thin, ruby film coating the engraved crystal. "I must congratulate you, my dear. A most unusual acquisition."

"He is hardly that, Gydapen."

"No?" The eyebrows lifted over the small, shrewd eyes. "Then what? Perhaps you will tell me, my friend."

"I merely escorted the lady, my lord," said Dumarest. "She needed someone to handle her raft. I understood the matter was Council business."

"Of course. Council business. Naturally." Gydapen gestured and a servant handed Dumarest a goblet of wine. Another and he departed leaving the three alone in the large hut. The interior was soft with delicate furnishings, rugs covering the floor, lanterns of colored glass hanging from the roof. At night it would be a warm, snug, comfortable place. One end would house the place where the mercenary slept. The other would contain stores, luxuries, wines and dainties to soften the rigors of the desert. "Your health, Earl!"

"Your health, my lord!"

Ceremoniously they drank, neither doing more than wet his lips and, watching them, Lavinia thought of two beasts of prey, circling, wary, neither willing to yield the advantage. Gydapen who owned land and commanded the loyalty of retainers, who had the protection of a great Family, who held the destiny of Zakym in the palm of his hand. And the other, alone, owning nothing, a traveller who searched for a dream.

But, watching them, she wondered why she had ever thought of Gydapen as a man worthy to sire her sons.

"The Council," he said again. "They think it right to send a woman without invitation, to land, to rob, to act the thief and spy. A woman whom I hold in high regard. Tell me, Earl, what do you think of such a Council?"

"They do what they can, my lord."

"As do we all. And, while I think about it, you have something belonging to Gnais, I think. The laser you struck from his hand. Thank you." He beamed as Dumarest dropped the weapon into his extended palm. "You made him look foolish. He will not relish that."

Lavinia said, abruptly, "Gydapen, for God's sake let's put an end to this! What are you doing? The guns? The men firing them at targets! Everything!"

"You saw?" Gydapen shrugged, his face expressionless, but his eyes moved to Dumarest. "Yet what did you see? Men training to protect me in case of need. Your own actions show that I have reason for such protection. You land, you order my own men to load your raft with goods which you know belong to me. Naked, outright theft. Are you proud of what your friends on the Council have made you do, Lavinia? Is it pleasant to know yourself for what you are?"

He was provoking her, hoping for an outburst of temper and the betrayal of secrets, but already she had said too much and knew it.

Quietly she said, "If you owe loyalty to the Council you will abide by their decision. The Pact is not to be broken. Must not be broken. Surely you can see that? What can you hope to gain by alienating the Sungari? Even if your mine shows profit what good can it do you if they turn against us?"

"Good?" Gydapen smiled and shrugged and toyed with his wine. "You are young, my dear. Innocent in the ways of commerce and men. But you are not drinking. Empty your goblet and permit me to refill it. You too, Earl. It is a good vintage. The best of this decade."

"I would enjoy it more, my lord, if I knew your intentions towards us."

"The direct question." Gydapen set down his glass and smiled with apparent pleasure but his eyes, Dumarest noticed, did not smile. "I admire you for putting it. You have strength and determination, qualities I can always use, but enough of that. Let us concentrate on the question. The answer, I am pleased to say, is nothing."

"My lord?"

"He can do nothing," said Lavinia, harshly. "Not unless he wishes to turn every hand against him. Alcorus knows we are here. Suchong, Erason, the others. I am on Council business. The guns were declared unlawful. You, Earl, did only as I ordered. He—"

"Could punish you for being a thief!" Gydapen looked at the hand he had slammed against the table then smiled. "What is the Council to me or to any Lord or Lady of Zakym? The guns are mine and will remain so. I do as I please and none will stop me. If they try I shall know what to do."

"You would kill your own?"

"I will defend what is mine. What is mine, Lavinia, and could be ours. Yes, my dear, could still be ours." Rising he extended his hands. "Let us forget this foolishness. You were curious, that I understand. Perhaps you are also ambitious. If so you will understand me better when I tell you that I, also, am ambitious."

He was, she realized, utterly sincere. At that moment if nothing else he spoke the naked truth. Then again he was smiling, leading them towards the door, opening it and ushering them towards the raft which rested, empty now, before the hut.

As it rose she said, "Earl, what did you think of him?"

"He's dangerous."

"True, but honest in certain ways don't you think?"

Dumarest said, flatly, "No madman is ever honest other than to his own delusions. How did he catch you?"

"I was wandering around with that man who met us when Gydapen appeared. I think he must have been here all the time."

A risk impossible to avoid. Had he been absent the guns would have been loaded and lifted away—now they had betrayed their intention. Yet he had permitted them to depart. Why?

Lavinia shrugged when he asked. "You heard him, Earl. There was nothing else he could have done."

"No," he corrected. "I heard you telling him that."

"It's the same thing."

To her, perhaps, but Dumarest recognized the difference. He looked at the sky. The suns were lowering towards the horizon, the discs merging, a haze softening the terrain below. The time of delusia when things were not exactly as they seemed and mistakes could easily be made.

Lavinia was at the controls. She looked beyond him as Dumarest touched her shoulder, her eyes vacant, her lips moving a little as if in silent conversation. Then, as he touched her again, she shuddered and leaned towards him.

"Charles! Charles, my dearest, why did—Earl!"

"What is the shortest way back to your castle?"

"South-west by west. The compass—"

"Over high ground?"

"Yes. The Iron Mountains run far back and there are some high peaks."

Together with crevasses and precipices and ledges which could crumble beneath the weight of a foot. Bad country but, it being late, it was natural she would have taken the route.

"Earl!" She caught at his arm as he altered the direction the vehicle was taking. "We'll never get back in time!"

"Does it matter? What about the stop-overs?"

"Yes." Her grip relaxed as she thought about it. "Yes, I suppose we could spend the night in one. But they aren't plentiful in this region. We'll have to rise high so as to spot where to land."

Rise high, very high, so high that nothing would be left of them or the raft if they crashed.

"Drop!" he snapped. "Fast!"

"Earl! What—"

"Do it! Get to the ground! Move!"

The engine was housed in a humped compartment. As Lavinia tilted the raft to send it gliding downwards to the misted terrain below Dumarest ripped at the casing, tearing away the thin metal with his knife, squinting as he peered inside. A grey cylinder rested against the engine, a cylinder which shouldn't have been there. He probed at it, eased it free and then, obeying the instinct which had saved him so often before, threw himself back and down.

The explosion was small, a dull report which caused the raft to judder and sent a puff of acrid yellow smoke from the engine compartment. Opened, it had lessened the damage, but it was still enough.

Dumarest heard Lavinia scream as the raft tilted. He rolled across the floor, felt the rail press against his shoulders and stabbed down with the knife, sending the blade slicing into the thin metal of the side. A hold to which he clung as the raft tilted still further, throwing him so that his body hung in space, only his grip on the knife and on the rail itself saving him from being hurled to the ground below.

"Level!" He yelled. "Level the raft!"

The woman, strapped into her seat, fought the controls, hair a tumbled mass over her face and eyes. The vehicle spun, lifted, dropped to spin again as if it were a falling leaf caught by sportive winds. Without power, supported only by the residual energy in the anti-grav units, the raft was little more than a mass of inert metal.

But still it had shape. A flat surface to act as a wing, permanent stabilizers fed from emergency sources, an aerodynamic balance which, with skill, gave a modicum of control.

Dumarest felt the strain on his arms lessen, a sudden blow as the edge of the raft hit against his stomach, then he was falling back into the body, sprawled, his knife ripped free and stabbed into the deck to provide another hold. Painfully, every muscle tense, he crawled to where the woman sat at the controls.

"Earl!" Her voice was high, strained with fear. "I can't handle it! We're going to crash! To crash!"

His arms closed around her as he locked his thighs around the chair on which she sat. His hands knocked hers aside as he took over control.

"Earl!"

"Crouch low. Bend your head into your lap. Rest your hands over the back of your neck. Turn into a ball if you can."

He stared at the swing and turn of the ground below. At the last moment, if able, he would release her straps and give her the best chance he could. Now, all he could do for the both of them, was to try and send the wrecked raft towards a slope, to keep it level, to let it skid instead of slamming against the rock and soil.

"How close?" Her voice was muffled but she had recovered her composure. "Earl, how close?"

"Brace yourself."

He dropped one hand to the release and freed her of the restraints. A hill loomed before them and he rugged, praying that the explosion hadn't totally destroyed the emergency units, that the hull would take the strain, that something, anything, would give them that little extra to clear the summit.

A gust of wind saved them. A vagrant blast which caught the prow of the raft, lifted it the essential fraction, letting it drop only after they had cleared the jagged peak. Below rolled a steep slope studded with massive boulders, mounded with accumulated soil tufted by patches of vegetation.

Like a stone thrown over water the raft bounced and skidded, metal tearing with harsh raspings, fragments ripped free to litter the slope. A mount flung them into the air, a dip lay beyond, a boulder which smashed like a hammer into the prow of the raft, to send them both hurtling forward, to part, to land with a stunning impact, to roll and finally to come to rest.

Dumarest stirred, feeling the ache of strained muscles, a warm wetness on the side of his face. A questing hand lowered stained with red, the blood welling from a gash in his scalp. With an effort he turned and sat upright, fighting the nausea which gripped him and sent the terrain wheeling in sickening spirals.

When it had passed he looked around. Behind him rested stone, a rock against which he had been thrown, the force of landing softened by the vegetation on which he lay. Sharp thorns and jagged stones had ripped the plastic of his tunic exposing the glint of metal mesh buried within. A defense which had saved him from cruel lacerations but had done nothing to save him from ugly bruises.

But he was alive, intact, dazed a little, suffering minor injuries but that was all. His luck had not deserted him.

And Lavinia's had not deserted her.

She lay in a shallow dell, a place thick with soft grasses, shrubs like springs which had taken her weight and eased the final part of her landing. She was unconscious, a lump beneath the mane of her hair but, as Dumarest discovered after examining her body, she was free of broken bones.

Rising he looked around. The suns were low, the air holding a peculiar hush as if strained with the energies of an imminent storm. But there were no clouds and little wind.

Walking back to the ruin of the raft he found his knife, used it to slash a reedy plant and collected a handful of pale sap which he used to bathe the woman's face.

"Earl?" Her eyelids fluttered. "Earl—what happened? Earl!"

"Steady!" His hand was firm on her shoulder. "Sit up if you can." He waited as she obeyed, staring with eyes free of suffused blood. A good sign—the chances were small she had a concussion. "Any internal pain? No? Good. Can you stand up and take a few steps?" He relaxed as she did as asked. At least she was mobile and he was freed of the necessity of taking care of a maimed and helpless person.

"Earl! Your face!"

"It's nothing." He collected more sap and washed the blood from his temple and cheek. The sap held a thin, sweet flavor and he drank a little. "Is any of this vegetation good to eat?"

"It won't hurt you but it contains no nourishment."

As he had expected, but at least it would fill their bellies in case of need. Lavinia stared her horror as he mentioned it.

"Earl, you can't be serious. We can't stay in the open. We have to find shelter before it's dark."

"Here?" He looked around, seeing nothing but the barren slope of the hill, the wreck of the raft.

"We must! Earl, we must!"

"Because of your bogey-men?"

"The Sungari! Earl, for God's sake believe me! If we are in the open at night we'll never see the dawn!"

Valid or not her terror was real. Dumarest looked at her, recognizing her near-panic, her incipient hysteria.

Quietly he said, "In that case we'll have to find somewhere to spend the night. Look around for a place while I go back to the raft."

"Why, Earl? What good can it do? The thing is a wreck."

But one which held sharp scraps of metal, wire, fabric, ribs—all things which could spell survival in a wilderness.

Dumarest examined it. The floor had been of metal covered with a coarsely woven fabric held with strips. He ripped them away, lifted the material and slashed it free with his knife. A coil of wire followed, some rods, a section of foil which he rolled into an awkward bundle. By the time he had finished the suns were resting on the horizon and Lavinia was desperate.

"I can't find a place, Earl. There aren't any caves. I don't even know in which direction the nearest stop-over is. The Sungari—Earl!"

He dropped his burden and held her in his arms until the quivering had stopped and she was calm again.

"If we can't find a place to stay then we'll make one." He gestured at the things he had assembled. "Need it be strong? Do the Sungari actually attack? Are they large or what?"

She didn't know as he had expected. Her fear was born of rumor and whispered convictions of a knowledge based on a lack of evidence. But, unless he were to end with an insane woman on his hands, he had to pander to her delusion.

As they worked she said, "Why couldn't we have used the wreck? Couldn't it have been easier?"

"No." Dumarest adjusted the fabric which he had stretched over the curved rods and lashed with wire. Rocks surrounded the crude tent and now he covered it with a thin layer of sand. "It was too big," he explained. "Too heavy to move and too awkward to seal. And I don't want to be there when they come looking for us."

"Looking?" Her eyes widened, filled with purple from the dying light. "Who? Gydapen?"

"A clever man." Dumarest dusted more sand over the shelter. "He knew you would be eager to get back home and, if we'd crashed over the Iron Mountains, we'd have stood no chance. He ever guessed that you might suspect him and head for a stop-over but, as you said, you'd have to ride high to spot one. Either way he couldn't lose."

"The explosion," she said, dully. "He sabotaged the raft."

"Which is why he insisted that we take wine with him and kept us busy with his cat and mouse game. He needed time to set the bomb and he wanted it to be late when we left." Dumarest looked at the woman. "He wanted to kill you," he said, evenly. "And he will want to be certain you are dead."

Would already be dead if it hadn't been for him. Lavinia had a sickening vision of herself, broken, bloodied, the prey for scavengers. It had been so close! If Dumarest hadn't suspected, hadn't acted when he had—and even then it had been close.

She felt a momentary weakness and closed her eyes, thankful she wasn't alone, thankful too that it was Dumarest with her and not Roland or Alcorus or even Charles when alive. Charles—how ignorant she had been! And Gydapen —how stupid!

She heard the rasp and scrape of stone against steel and turned to see Dumarest squatting, knife in hand, sparks flying from the blade. Some finely fretted material lay before him on a small heap of whittled twigs. A nest which caught the sparks and held them as, gently, he blew them to flame.

A fire—but why?

Watching, she saw him feed the glow, building it to a blaze which he lifted with the aid of metal torn from the roll of foil and carried to a place between rocks well to one side. More foil, the rest of the roll, made a humped shape behind it.

"A decoy!" Finally she understood. "If anyone should come they will see it and think we are with it. But no one will come at night, Earl."

"Can you be sure of that?"

"How could they spot the wreck?"

"There are ways." He added more fuel to the blaze. Smoke wreathed his face making it cruel in the crimson light. "We found the bomb but a tracking device could have been fitted."

"They won't come at night," she insisted. "Not even Gydapen."

Perhaps not, but the man wasn't alone and mercenaries had few compunctions as to how they earned their pay. Gnais would be free of the planetary phobia concerning the dark. Infra-red devices could be available to track down the living if they had escaped death in the wreck. The fire would confuse such apparatus and mask their own body heat.

Things he explained. Lavinia listened, nodding when he had finished.

"You're clever, Earl. Now, for God's sake, let us get out of the night!"

Chapter FIFTEEN

The shelter was small with barely enough room for them both. Without light, the walls pressing close, Dumarest was reminded too strongly of a tomb. Carefully parting the opening of the flap he looked outside.

The suns had vanished, the sky now blazed with stars, the pale, ghostly luminescence painting the rocks, the tufted vegetation with frosted silver. The glow of the fire was a dull reflection caught and dimmed by facing rocks. A ruby nimbus of shifting light in which figures moved in an intricate saraband.

A man in armor, gilt and tinsel over red and green, a helmet framing a skull in the eyeholes of which worms crawled and lifted heads which sighed with ancient yearnings. A fancy, gone even as seen, replaced by another which spun like a pinwheel, semi-transparent, a cut-out which danced, a face filled with bulging eyes. Red stained the mouth and ears, more the nose and cheeks. Tears of blood which dripped and left a trail in which paper-thin fingers dabbled and rose to trace symbols on the air.

Chagney!

Wheeling on his eternal journey among the stars.

His eyes bulged at the sight of unimaginable glories. His blood was a benediction to all who had spilled their lives in the void. His appearance was an accusation.

As was the woman with hair of flame.

Had he loved her, the real woman, or merely the shell she had worn?

Had she known and, knowing, taken a subtle revenge?

Kalin—had she lied?

Dumarest closed his eyes, shutting out the imaginary figures, feeling the tension at the base of his skull, the inward pressure. Something . . . something . . . but it was so long ago and now was not the time to remember.

Now was the time of the Sungari.

"Earl!" Lavinia was beside him, pressing close, her breath warm against his cheek. "Close the opening—please!"

Had they never built strong rooms fitted with thick windows? Were they afraid of the madness such rooms would bring?

"Earl! Please!"

Dumarest drew in his breath, shuddering, conscious of the ache at the base of his skull, the pressure. The hallucinations had been too real, too accusing. Fragments of the past, enhanced, given the acid sauce of hindsight, the torment of what might have been. A blur of images of which only a few had been prominent but, behind those few, ghostly yet horribly alive, had thronged others.

A man lived every second of every hour since the time of his birth and each of those seconds held all that had happened to and around him.

A vastness of experience. An inexhaustible supply of terror and pain and hopeless yearning. An infinity of doubt and indecision, of ignorance known and forceably accepted, of frustration and hate and cruelty and fear.

A morass in which glowed the fitful gleams of transient joy.

Each man, within his skull, carried a living hell.

Watching, Dumarest had seen it.

"Earl?" Lavinia touched his face and felt the sweat which wet her fingers. Felt too the little quivers which ran through him so that he trembled like a beast which had been run too hard for too long. She pushed back his hair, touching

151

the gash on his scalp, the sting of the salt on her hand a pain which, meeting, diminished the rest. "For God's sake! Earl!"

He was trapped, buried, stifling. Sand clogged his lungs and mountains weighed his limbs. He threshed, tore at the opening, jerked it aside and lunged through to roll on the stoney ground to rise, to stare wide-eyed at the stars.

Earth!

Which was the sun which warmed Earth?

"Come back, you fool!" Lavinia screamed from within the confines of the shelter. "Come back! The Sungari—hurry!"

It was already too late.

Dumarest heard a thin, high pitched whine, the drone of something which passed, the lash of air against his face, his eyes. It came again and he dropped, feeling a jerk at his hair, something which touched his scalp and burned like fire.

Against the stars there was a shimmer, a blur. Night mist falling or something else?

Then again the whine, something which struck his shoulder, to rip the plastic and tear at the metal beneath. A blow which bruised and hurt and shocked him from his daze. Alerted, his instinct to survive replaced conscious thought.

He dropped, felt the whine of disturbed air slash through the spot where he'd been standing, rolled to see sand and dirt plume inches from his face. The shelter was close and he dived towards it, seeing the opening part a little, the pale glimmer of a face. It backed as he advanced, making room for him to pass through, legs kicking, his boot hitting something and being hit in turn. Jerking up his knees he drove the edge of his hand against something which shimmered, again at something else which droned.

"Earl!"

"Something to block the opening! Quickly!"

The fabric was too thin. He held it, smashing at it with his fist as it bulged, wedging the fabric handed to him against it, lashing it with strands of wire. Above, on the roof of the shelter, something scrabbled, rasping, making eerie chitterings.

"It's too thin," she whispered. "Too thin."

And he had been too confident of her mistaken fear of the dark. It had been no mistake. Thinking so had almost cost him his life.

"They'll get us!" Her voice rose a little. "They'll break in."

"No." He reached out and found her. She was naked, the fabric she had passed to him the clothing she had ripped from her body. "They won't break in," he soothed. "Not now we're out of sight."

Out of sight their scent masked, but that need have nothing to do with it. Sight alone would have been enough. The fury of the attack had caused it to last after he had vanished from view. A delayed action which even now was ending.

As he listened the scrabbling faded, the chittering died.

"Earl?"

"It's over. All we need do now is wait."

Wait as she moved against him, soft and warm and with a femininity which could not be denied. A burning, demanding creature of passion who held him and touched him and sent her lips questing over his cheeks, his eyes, lingering on his mouth until his arms closed around her. A cleansing, human thing who washed the fragments of delusion from his mind and filled the tiny shelter with a heat which rose to engulf them both.

Which ebbed to flood again at the approach of dawn.

Dumarest stirred, looking at the tumble of hair against his shoulder, the face it stranded, the eyes closed, the lips swollen, the whole lax in satiation. The morning light was dim as it percolated through the fabric, brightening as he cleared the opening, becoming a pale flood as he pushed aside the flaps.

Crawling outside he rose and stretched. His hands stung and he saw the knuckles scored with shallow wounds, the fingers dark with blood. More dried blood matted his hair and traced a pattern on his face. His boots were torn, the pants showed long gouges as if sharp knives had slashed at the material. On the sanded surface of the shelter the grains were fanned into intricate designs.

The fire he had lit had died, a patch of ash marring

153

the sand with greyish blackness. He gathered fuel and lit another, feeding it gently, adding leaves and tufts of greenery so that a thin column of smoke rose into the air. A column which thickened and turned an oily black as he fed slivers of plastic into the flames.

"Earl?" Lavinia had woke and dressed herself in the torn shred of her clothing, the gleam of nacreous flesh showing through the rents as she crawled from the shelter and straightened. Her eyes, like her lips, were puffed a little, soft with tender memory, the pleasure so recently enjoyed. "Why the fire? A signal?"

"If anyone is looking for us I don't want them to waste time." Dumarest looked at the sky, squinting, the dried blood on his face giving him the appearance of a savage warrior.

"But last night you were worried about Gydapen finding us," she pointed out. "That's why you built the fire as a decoy."

"That was last night."

"And now?"

"We're stranded in the wilderness. We need food and water and shelter against the night. We have no maps and no compass. Can you guide us to safety? Get us to a stop-over before dark?" He shrugged as she made no answer. "If all else fails we'll have to try, but I don't think it will be necessary. Gydapen will want to check that we are dead. The fire will tell whoever's looking that we're not. He'll land. When he does we'll take his raft."

If anyone came. If he landed. If he could be overpowered —Dumarest made it sound so simple.

"We need water," she said. "Something to wash in. Your face and hands are covered in blood." As was her cheek, her shoulders and back, the swell of her breasts. Blood from Dumarest's injured hands and face. "And I'm hungry."

"We've nothing to eat."

"Maybe I could find something. There could be berries and roots. I'll look around."

"You'll get back into the shelter and stay there," he said, flatly. "Sleep if you can but don't come out for any reason. Movement is easily spotted from the air."

154

The tiny space was a mess, the sand torn with the fury of their passion, splotched with blood. To one side something glinted as it rested against an edge of the shelter. Dumarest picked it up. It was a foot long, wings now broken, scaled body now crushed to ooze a thin ichor. Six legs ended in vicious claws. Two huge eyes glowed like flawed gems. Gaping mandibles were serrated like razor-edged saws. A streamlined creature, armed and armored, which could fly and strike and be as effective as a missile.

"What is it?" Lavinia frowned as she studied it. "How did it get in here?"

He had carried it with him when he had dived into the shelter. He had crushed it, rolled on it, broken it with a slash of his palm. Had the final attack been to recover it? If any others had died they were not to be seen.

"The Sungari?" Lavinia glanced at Dumarest. "Is that what it is?"

A part but never the whole. No Pact could be made with such a thing. It was an extension as a bee was to a hive. A nocturnal flyer programmed to attack anything in the shape of a human. A collector of food which scoured the terrain during the hours of darkness.

Somewhere, buried deep, must repose the intelligences which directed it. The true Sungari.

Throwing aside the creature Dumarest said, "Get into the shelter now and wait. And remember what I said—don't leave it for any reason."

"And you, Earl?"

"I'll be close."

Meekly she obeyed, finding a pleasure in having decisions made for her, orders which she had to obey. The day brightened and she heard small scuffling sounds followed by silence. Through the opening she could see the thick column of smoke rising upwards. A shape rested beside it, manlike, still. Dumarest sleeping? Lying quietly as he tended the fire?

Turning she looked upwards along the slope of the hill towards the wreck. The summit traced a sharp edge across the sky, shadows like paint at the foot of rocks and tufted vegetation. The sky was clear, traced only with the thin

155

strands of high-flying mist which gleamed at times like silver lace.

Her thirst increased and hunger caused her stomach to ache. She moved, pressing herself against the sand, forgetting physical misery in memory of the night. Never before had it been so wonderful. Never again would she need to envy another woman her experience of love.

Restlessly she turned, conscious of the heat, the cramped confines of the shelter. Beside the fire the shape lay as before, unmoving, a gleam coming from the ripped fabric. It vanished as she turned her head; a mirror now throwing its reflected beam elsewhere. How could Dumarest remain so still?

Softly she called to him. "Earl. Earl, are you asleep?"

The words died in the silence and, suddenly, she was convinced that he was dead or gone and that she was alone.

"Earl!"

The fabric at the opening parted as she thrust herself forward. Twisting she looked up the slope of the hill and saw the bulk of the wreck, the sharp line of the summit, the dark shape of the raft which hung above.

For a second she froze then jerked her head back into the shelter, praying that the lone occupant of the vehicle hadn't seen her. It was the mercenary, Gnais, leaning forward as he sat at the controls, head moving from side to side as he scanned the area.

The raft dropped lower, its shadow passing before her, the thin whine of the engine surprisingly loud as it hovered close to the column of smoke.

"Hey, down there! Is anyone around?" His harsh voice grated through the air. "You by the fire—you hurt or something?"

Watching she saw the figure twitch a little. An arm moved and, from where he leaned over the edge of the raft, Gnais lifted his laser and fired.

Earl!

Lavinia tasted blood as her teeth dug into her lower lip. Her hands, clenched, drove nails into her palms and she felt physically ill. Dumarest dead! Murdered! Slaughtered like a stricken beast!

Vomit rose in her throat as she crouched, trembling in the shelter. A helpless animal as she watched the raft swing slowly over the area to finally come to rest a few yards from the wreck. The mercenary, casual, stepped from the vehicle and walked towards the fire.

"One down," she heard him mutter. "But where's the other? The woman?"

He spun as she moved, the laser lifting, freezing in his hand as he saw her face framed in the opening. Smiling he took a step towards her, another, a third.

"Come out, my dear, I won't hurt you. I saw the smoke and came to investigate. What happened? Were you attacked? Are you hurt?" His arm gestured upwards towards his raft. "I've water and food if you need it. Come out now, there's no need to be afraid."

A liar and she knew it. He would take her and use her and leave her body on the sand to be disposed of by scavengers. She could read it in his eyes, in the moist anticipation of his mouth. A vileness who, armed, was confident he could do as he liked without opposition. One who gestured with increasing impatience.

"Don't be foolish. Come out of there. I won't hurt you. Come on now." His voice thinned, became a snarl. "Move, you bitch! Get into the open before I teach you a lesson. What'll it be? Some channels burned into your back? A breast charred? Holes in your buttocks? Come out or I'll burn you!"

He meant it, wanted to do it, would probably take greater pleasure from the sadistic play than if she yielded meekly to his desires.

Yet she couldn't move.

Couldn't!

"Your last chance," he snapped. "No? Well, you asked for it."

Deliberately he fired. One of the rods supporting the flimsy roof of the shelter fused and fell to one side, fabric and sand falling to coat her body and soil her hair. Again the laser spat its beam and she screamed as fire touched her thigh to sear her flesh.

"No! Don't! Please don't!"

Rising she saw his face, the eyes which widened to gloat over the rents in her clothing, the flesh beneath.

"A beauty! You'll give me pleasure before you die!"

He took a step towards her, another—then jerked as if hit in the back. His head reared back, face towards the sky, lowering as, mouth open, he tried to scream. Blood came before the sound, a thick spout of crimson which frothed like a fountain to splash on the sand, forming a pool into which he fell.

Numbly Lavinia looked at him, at the hilt of the knife which rose between his shoulders.

At the near-naked figure of Dumarest who stood behind a rock.

"Earl! Earl, you—thank God you're alive!"

"Are you hurt?" He came forward to kick aside the fallen laser and stood watching her as she shook with reaction and relief. "He fired at you. Are you hurt?"

"A small burn. It's nothing. But you—Earl, I saw him kill you."

"Not quite," he said dryly. "I set up a dummy. It's an old trick. I had a thread fastened to the arm. When it moved he fired and thought as you did. He wouldn't have landed until he was certain there was no danger."

A trick—the whole thing had been planned, but why hadn't he told her? Lavinia swallowed, remembering how she had felt, the terror, the sick, horrible fear.

"You should have told me."

"And you shouldn't have moved. I warned you to remain still. If you had he wouldn't have seen you." Dumarest stooped and tugged out his knife, wiping the blade on the dead man's clothing. Rising he saw her face. "Are you all right?"

"Yes." She sucked air into her lungs, remembering who she was, her position. The Lady of Belamosk should not be a coward and yet she had known fear. A word, a hint even, and she would have been able to retain her composure. Instead of which she had almost begged.

Begged!

"There's probably water in his raft," said Dumarest. "And maybe something for that burn. Wait here and I'll get it."

"There's no need." At least she could salvage something of her pride. And, woman-like, take a minor revenge. Looking at the dead man she said, meaningfully, "The knife. You threw it. You stabbed him in the back."

"Of course," said Dumarest. "What else?"

Chapter SIXTEEN

~~~~~~~~~~~~~~~~

Roland said, "I don't know how to thank you, Earl. There are no words. Lavinia—well, you understand."

More than he guessed, to Dumarest it was obvious the man was in love with the woman. An emotion he managed to hide or she was too blind to see. It would not be the first time that close association masked the truth.

Leaning back he looked around the room into which he had been led. They had arrived late in the afternoon, beating curfew by an hour, attendants ushering them to baths and food and rest. Now, toying with his wine, Dumarest waited for the other to speak what was on his mind.

"Gydapen. Are you sure he tried to kill you?"

"Yes."

"But the mercenary—"

"Was a paid tool." Dumarest added, acidly, "You find it hard to believe that a noble of this world could descend to murder?"

"On Zakym it is unusual. A challenge, yes, followed by a duel if satisfaction cannot otherwise be obtained, but murder—" He broke off, shaking his head, a man no longer certain of his world. And yet he had travelled and must know that not all cultures followed the niceties of procedure as to the display of courage, the duelist's code—idiocies for which Dumarest had no patience. "And there is no doubt as to his arming men?"

"Ask Lavinia."

"Ask her what?" She entered the room and came towards them, helping herself to wine, sipping before looking from one to the other. Now, washed, her hair neatly dressed, her body clothes in fine material, she wore her composure like a cloak. "Earl, I must apologize, I was rude."

He said nothing, waiting.

"I was angry and sneered at your having killed that man the way you did. You were right. He deserved no warning, no chance to defend himself. He was filth!"

"He was dangerous," said Dumarest. "An armed man always is. And I was in no mood to play games." He looked at Roland. "Are you?"

"Games? Me?"

"The Council if you prefer. Those whose job it is to keep the peace on this planet. Those who have the authority and so should have the responsibility. Or have you no objection to war?"

"Earl!" Lavinia stared at him, her eyes wide. "What are you talking about? War? What war?" Then, thinking she understood, she nodded. "Of course. Once he breaks the Pact the Sungari will attack."

"The Sungari don't enter into it," said Dumarest. "At least not as far as Gydapen is concerned. He has no intention of breaking the Pact."

"But his new mine?"

"What mine? Do you dig holes with guns?" He stared at them, baffled by their innocence, the cultural drag which made it impossible for them to comprehend. "Don't you understand even yet what Gydapen intends? Lavinia, try!"

She stared at him. "Earl?"

"He told you. He admitted he was ambitious. He has travelled and knows what can be done by men of determination and drive. He has men and guns and who is to stand against him? Conquest, woman! Gydapen intends to become the sole ruler of this world!"

"No!" Roland shook his head. "He can't. The Council will never permit it."

"The Council will be dead."

"But he will be stopped—"

"By whom?"

"The Families. The retainers. We, that is, there must—" Roland broke off, helpless. "Lavinia?"

She said, "He wants me. If it will bring peace he can have me. I will make the surrender of the guns the price of my agreement to wed."

Dumarest said, coldly, "He tried to kill you, have you forgotten? Are you a child to value your body so highly? Marriage? He doesn't have to marry, he can take. As Gnais would have taken. Don't be a fool, woman, this isn't a game. Gydapen is gambling for the ownership of a world. What is a woman against that?"

Nothing as she was willing to admit. A momentary fire, a passion, the easing of lust, the use of a toy—unless love was present what use to talk of sacrifice?

"Earl, what can we do?"

"You have little choice. It's too late to send for arms and hire mercenaries to use them. Too late to train your retainers. The Sungari, perhaps, but gaining their cooperation will take time and you have no time."

"So?"

Dumarest said, "Once, on a far world, I heard a story. It could be true. There was a man who sat at the head of a great House. Those under him were ambitious and friends came to warn him of danger. He said nothing but stepped into his garden. In it were flowers, some taller than others. Still remaining silent he slashed the head off the tallest bloom with his cane. Those with him knew exactly what he meant and what to do."

"Kill," said Roland. "Gydapen?"

"Gydapen." Dumarest finished his wine. "Before he learns that we're still alive."

This time they approached from the south, riding low, skimming over the hills, hugging the valleys, invisible to men and machines which searched the upper sky. Three rafts, each with a driver, hand-picked young men who could shoot and were eager for adventure. More rode with them;

five in Roland's vehicle, four with Lavinia, four with Dumarest. Numbers only, shapes to be seen against the skyline, weight which would provide a distraction.

Only half of them were armed with weapons culled from the trophy room of the castle; rifles used for sport, not war, crossbows which could fire a bolt as lethal as a bullet if aimed true, a clutter of knives and ornate spears.

Pathetic things to set against machine rifles, but those rifles could change hands.

And the plan was simple.

Roland to break shortly and gain height. To lift and ride high as he headed directly towards the camp. There he would land and make a noise, demanding to see Gydapen, asking questions, worried about Lavinia and her continued absence. The men with him, even though crudely armed, would be a problem and would need to be handled with caution unless Gydapen was ready to make his move.

Lavinia would come in from the direction of the firing range, dropping as close to a small party of armed men as she could, using her authority to demand a momentary obedience, a chance to overpower them, disarm them, to move in with the captured weapons.

Dumarest would work alone.

He touched the driver on the shoulder as they neared a ridge. Beyond lay a slope, a stretch of rugged ground and then the arid waste. To cross it on foot would take too long but the chances of the raft remaining unobserved were small.

"Steady," he warned. "Don't veer. Just keep drifting lower as if you were riding a descending wind and were too busy talking to notice it. You two get ready to jump with me."

They nodded, eyes anxious, fighting the temptation to look over the side.

Dumarest looked at the sky. The suns were close and edging closer. Soon now they would merge and delusia begin. With luck those on watch would be talking to the departed. They would discount distant figures, could even mistake the raft for a piece of the delusion. Small gains, but every one mattered as they couldn't attack at night.

And, this time, there would be no attempt to bluff.

"Ready!" Dumarest looked down, judging time and distance. Ahead and below ran a shallow crevice which reached almost to the edge of the waste ground. Boulders strewed the ground between its end and the area of the huts. "The crevice! Get into it!"

The driver was skilled. Expertly he dropped the raft until it moved slowly over the bottom of the crevice.

"Now!" Dumarest touched the others on their shoulders. "Drop!"

He was over the side before they had moved, not waiting to see if they would obey. He hit, rolling, coming to a halt beside a stunted shrub. The others fell more heavily, one crying out at the snap of bone."

"My leg!"

It was a clean break and Dumarest bound it, setting the limb and using the haft of a spear as a splint. The raft had gone, turning, rising, veering as it lifted to head well to one side. There it would drop again, to lift, to move on and repeat the maneuver. Apparently sowing a line of men in an arc about the camp, finally to come to rest with those remaining ready to do their share.

"Sir?" The injured man looked at Dumarest. "I'm sorry."

"You couldn't help it."

"My foot turned on a stone. I should have been more careful."

An obvious fact but one useless to emphasize. To the other Dumarest said, "Stay with him. Try and get up to the edge of the crevice and, when you hear firing, begin to shoot. Aim high. I want noise not casualties but if anyone attacks you then get them first."

"Yes, sir. I—"

The man broke off, his face turning blank. Then, as Dumarest watched, his lips began to move and he smiled and nodded to empty air. Delusia. To him someone would be standing there, talking and smiling in turn.

Cradling his rifle Dumarest ran down the crevice. Before him a shrub blurred and became a tall, regal figure with glinting, golden hair. It vanished as he shook his head, conscious of the dull ache at the base of his skull, the pressure. It grew into a sudden burst of pain which sent him, sweating, to his knees and then, abruptly, was gone.

164

The wall of the crevice was loose, dirt and stone falling beneath hands and feet as he scrabbled his way up to the edge. The area beyond was deserted, Roland's raft slanting in to land, the men aboard leaning over the rail, displaying their weapons.

Dumarest began to run.

If the camp was properly guarded he would be seen and, if Gydapen had given the correct orders, met by a hail of bullets. But as yet the retainers were strangers to war, unblooded and reluctant to kill. Gydapen himself lacked experience and was, perhaps, over-confident. Gnais, the one man who would have known what to do, was dead.

Dumarest ran on.

The raft was low now and he could hear the thin sound of distant voices. The huts loomed ahead, the latrine closer then the rest. He reached it as the cookhouse door began to swing wide, flinging himself down, rolling to hide behind a loose hanging set to give protection against the wind.

He heard the sound of footsteps, the splash of running water, a grunt as someone set down the container he had just emptied into the trench.

"A hell of a job," he muttered. "Feldaye, you're lucky to be out of it. I know you warned me but what could I do? The Lord Gydapen Prabang ordered and what he wants he gets. You know that Martha got married to young Engep? Well, you can argue about that when you see her."

The muttering faded, a man talking to another who existed only in his memory. Rising Dumarest edged forward towards the cookhouse, threw the rifle on its roof and, taking a flying jump, followed it.

He landed like a cat, snatched up the weapon and moved down towards the end used as a storeroom. Lying flat he looked over the ridge of the roof.

Roland was still arguing, his arms gesticulating, those with him scowling at the others standing around. Dumarest looked at the sky, the suns were moving apart, the discs well separated and delusia, now already weak, would soon be over.

He looked back at the gathering. Gydapen was nowhere to be seen.

From the crowd a man said, loudly, "She is not here. You must leave."

"Not without the Lady Lavinia Del Belamosk!"

"You will leave." The man lifted his machine rifle. Already he was aware of the power it gave, the obedience it commanded. Soon it would come to dominate his life—if he lived that long.

Dumarest fired as the weapon levelled on Roland's slight figure.

He fired again as the man fell, finding another target, a third. The rifle he held was a sporting gun, well-balanced, the magazine holding fifteen cartridges, the universal sight throwing a point of red against the impact-point of the bullet.

Three down—why hadn't Roland seized their guns?

The raft lifted as machine rifle fire sent bullets to chew at the side and rear. Within the vehicle a man screamed, rearing, blood jetting from torn arteries. For a moment he hung as if painted against the sky then, as the force of his spring yielded to the pull of gravity, he toppled, to fall over the side, to land with a wet thud on the stoney ground.

More guns blasted at the raft and a man hung over the rail, one hand dangling, the entire lower jaw shot away so that he seemed to be lost in a ghastly paroxysm of laughter.

As the craft veered Dumarest adjusted his aim, fired, sent another bullet after the first, a stream which cut into the pack, sought out those with guns poised ready to fire and sent them into a broken, bloody heap. A blast of fire delivered with a cold precision in order to save the lives of those in the raft. One which drew attention to himself.

He heard shouts, the yell of orders and the pound of feet. The dormitory huts blocked his view, but he saw the barrel of a gun, and slid back down the roof as the ridge disintegrated and wasp-like hummings cut the air.

"On the roof!" The yell was hoarse. "He's on the roof!"

"Get him!"

The man gaped as Dumarest dropped to land before him. Before he could move the butt of the rifle had slammed against his jaw, the muzzle stabbing into the stomach of his companion, doubling the man before the stock cracked his skull.

Dumarest turned, saw the glint of metal at the corner of the hut and threw himself down and aside as the gun snarled and dirt plumed into little fountains. The rifle levelled, fired, sending chips flying from the edge of the building, fired again, driving the bullet through two walls and into the brain of the man behind. Reaching him Dumarest snatched up his gun.

The rifle was too long for easy maneuverability, too limited in fire-power. A precision instrument which had served its purpose. Life now would depend on speed, the ability to send a stream of fire to force others to take cover, the willingness to kill.

A man saw his face, recognized what it contained, and ran. Dumarest let him go. The door of a dormitory hut slammed open beneath his boot and he lunged into the building, firing, fragments spouting from shattered lamps, cups, the surface of the table. Water gushed from the smashed container—the only liquid spilled. The hut was deserted.

"Roland!"

Dumarest shouted as he reached the other door. It gave a good view of the space before the huts, the large building to one side. The raft was grounded before it, the sides perforated, the vehicle useless. Around it men lay in the sprawled postures of death. Others crawled or, too badly hurt to move, cried out for water. Smoke hazed the air but the firing had stopped.

"Roland!" Dumarest narrowed his eyes. The man could be dead or too badly hurt to answer. "Can you hear me? Roland!"

He caught a glimpse of movement at a window of the large building and ducked as a gun snarled, feeling the bite of splinters in his cheek, the brush of something which added another scar to his tunic. He fired in return, traversing the gun, blasting the window with a hail of missiles, releasing the trigger at a shape, torn beyond recognition, spun and slumped through the shattered opening.

"Roland!"

"Here, Earl." A hand lifted to signal. "That man in there had us pinned down. What's the position?"

A good question but Dumarest hesitated before answering.

The immediate danger was over, those who'd had guns were dead or hurt. Others had run and he guessed that if the large building held more men they would not be eager to show themselves.

But there would be more men, more guns, and they no longer held the advantage of surprise.

The key was Gydapen. If they could find and kill him they would be safe.

Roland gasped as Dumarest dropped at his side. He was pale, his blouse stained, blood on his cheek, but the stains were dirt and the blood not his own.

"Four dead," he reported. "Two in the first burst. The driver got it shortly after. The rest are too badly hurt to move. I hope that Lavinia had better luck than we did."

Dumarest tilted his head. There should have been firing, the echo of shots both from the edge of camp and the firing range. A few scattered reports came from where he had left the others but Lavinia's area remained silent.

"What now?" Roland licked his lips. "We're trapped, helpless should they decide to attack. They could crush us in seconds. Earl—"

"We're armed," snapped Dumarest. "We can fight back. They aren't used to that. All they've done so far is to shoot at targets. Firing at armed men is different. It takes getting used to. When I give the word we'll run to the large building. Get inside as fast as you can—it would be best to dive through the window. I'll cover you then you cover me. Don't bother to aim, just keep firing, while you do that they'll keep down. Ready? Go!"

The building was empty. Dumarest moved from room to room, kicking open the doors, returning to the chamber in which Gydapen had given him wine. From where he stood by the window Roland said, bleakly, "We've failed. We haven't killed Gydapen and we can't get away. It's only a matter of time before they get us."

Dumarest made no answer. He stared beyond the man at the space outside. At the raft which came drifting slowly towards the building in which they stood. At Lavinia standing in it.

Gydapen was at her side.

He was smiling, seemingly very calm, very assured, but his eyes darted from side to side, touching the wreck, the litter of dead, the shattered window.

Roland, careless, had shown himself.

"My Lord Acrae, this is a pleasure. Not one but two members of the Council coming to partake of my hospitality. But how do you account for the violence of your arrival? To shoot and kill my retainers—such an act needs explanation and redress. But perhaps you were unduly influenced by another? One who could be watching from shadows?" His face lost the smile and became savage. "If you are here, Dumarest, show yourself! If you care for the woman come into sight with empty hands."

He stood beside Lavinia, very close, one hand weighed with a laser, the other hidden behind her back. The fingers were locked in her hair and, suddenly, her faced jerked towards the sky.

"Dumarest!"

He moved to the window as Gydapen shouted and stood for a moment in full view then, throwing aside the gun, stepped over the sill. Roland followed him, breathing quickly, afraid, wanting to run and hide but driven by his pride to act the man.

Gydapen ignored him.

"You joined others and moved against me," he said to Dumarest. "Why? What harm have I done you?"

"You forget the raft, my lord."

"The work of Gnais. But I am being foolish—a mercenary needs no excuse to take sides. The pay is reason enough. Gnais—" He shrugged. "A failure. Such a man is better dead. And you have done more for me than he had. The attack could not have served me better. A prelude which has stiffened my men. Now they know a little of the harsh reality of war."

"Against the Sungari?" Lavinia made no effort to mask her contempt. "Gydapen, you are a fool!"

"And you are stupid." He released her and watched as she stepped from him to halt at the side of the raft. "What interest have I in the Sungari? They were an excuse, dust to throw in your eyes. As was my talk of marriage. Marriage!"

He smiled with an ugly twist of the lips. "Once I own this world I will need a consort worthy of my position. Not a child consumed by lust."

"A child?" Deliberately she inflated her chest, accentuating her unmistakable femininity. "Are you man enough even for that?"

"Enough, you bitch!"

"Yes, enough!" Her anger matched his own. "You're mad, Gydapen. Mad!"

As were all who fell victim to insane ambition, but it was never wise to tell them so. Dumarest said, quickly, "My lord, I admire your military skill. How did you capture the woman?"

"Luck," she said before he could answer. "He was inspecting his men and must have become suspicious. He attacked before we could move. We had no chance. I alone was left alive."

"Luck?" Dumarest raised his eyebrows. "I think it was other than that. A warning, perhaps? An instinct? Even so you are clever, my lord. It becomes obvious to me now that I have made a mistake. A wise man does not back the losing side."

"Earl!"

Gydapen ignored the woman as did Dumarest. He had edged a little to one side and took another step as, in the raft, Gydapen leaned forward. A small motion but one which increased the space between himself and Lavinia.

"You would be interested in fresh employment?"

"For a strong cause, my lord, yes."

"Mine is strong enough. I have men and arms and—" Gydapen broke off as if conscious he was saying too much. For a long moment he remained silent then, with a shrug said, "Well, why not? A man must eat and you have proved your worth. And what loyalty does a mercenary have other than to his own welfare. Yet I must have some proof that you would be reliable."

Dumarest said, "You would have my word."

"Which, probably, has never been broken." Gydapen lifted one foot and rested it on the edge of the raft. On it he rested the hand holding the laser. Around the vehicle, where they had dropped when it landed, his guards stood armed and watchful. "Yet you will permit me a little doubt. A word, an oath, such things are fragile. Deeds are something else." Then, without change of tone he said, "Kill Roland and the woman."

"My lord?"

"Kill them both and join my retinue."

Dumarest looked at the watching men. They were tense, unaware exactly of what was happening, but conscious they were witnessing something strange. The one nearest to him had a face dewed with sweat, more sweat liquid on the stock of the gun he held, muzzle high.

Gydapen said, sharply, "You hesitate?"

"A moment for thought, my lord. A man does not kill for nothing. My reward—"

"High rank in my army. High pay and what pleasures you choose to take." Gydapen lifted the laser, his knuckle white on the trigger. "Now obey!"

"Without a gun?"

"You have a knife. Use it!"

Sunlight glinted from the blade as Dumarest lifted it from his boot. Deliberately he turned it, causing it to flash, splinters of light which caught the eye and held the attention. Roland sucked in his breath as Dumarest moved towards him.

"Earl! For God's sake! You can't!"

"Scream," said Dumarest, softly. "Scream, you fool, then fall and lie still!"

He moved in, the blade circling around the other's uplifted hand, making a mockery of the pathetic defense. His arm straightened, slashed as the man shrieked, blood dulling the edge of the knife as he lifted it high.

On the sand Roland crouched, hands at his throat, falling to reveal the crimson gash. A shallow wound which had barely cut the skin but one which bled, accentuating the damage, looking ghastly as the man fell to one side, to twitch, to lay still.

"One down, my lord." Dumarest stepped towards the raft. "Now for the other. A pity to waste such beauty but your orders must be obeyed."

171

"A dog eating the filth of its master," she sneered. "You disgust me. Gydapen, you have chosen well."

He turned, smiling, his hand with the laser swinging wide, then, too late, he realized the mistake he had made, the danger he was in.

"No!"

His hand lifted as he yelled, finger closing as razor-edged steel hurtled through the air to hit, to bury itself in the hollow of his throat, to send him toppling forward vomiting blood on the dirt.

As he fell Dumarest moved, snatching the gun from the man he had marked, blasting the air and ground with its snarl and hail as he clamped his finger on the trigger. Smoke rose from the side of his head, the burning hair now quenched by the blood which laved the area. The sear of the laser was an angry furrow of red and black high above one ear. He looked a savage, blood-crazed avenger determined to kill.

The guards broke, throwing aside the weapons as they raced for the shelter of the huts.

"Earl!" He dropped the gun as Lavinia came running towards him from the raft. "You were wonderful! I guessed all along what you intended but, Gydapen, the fool, didn't guess all you wanted was a chance to get your knife before he could fire. Well, he's dead now and it's over."

"Yes," said Dumarest. "He's dead."

"And it's over," she repeated emphatically. "We'll have peace now."

A peace he could share.

It was in the promise of her eyes, her lips, the warmth of her body as she pressed herself close against him. A gentle time with good living and soft luxuries. A time to rest and think and make leisurely plans. The days would blend one into another and, at night, there would be the protection of strong buildings and the comfort of her love. He could hide here, take what was offered, forget the search for Earth. Find refuge, even, from the Cyclan.

A haven.

A haven of darkness. One free of the glittering torment of the stars.

"Earl?" Her lips were very close, very tempting. "You'll stay, Earl? For a while, at least, you'll stay?"

For a while—why not?

"Yes, Lavinia," he said. "I'll stay."

Presenting the saga of Earl Dumarest's search for Terra—the greatest work of a great science fiction writer:

☐ **JONDELLE by E. C. Tubb.** Dumarest's trail to Lost Terra leads through a city of paranoid kidnappers.
(#UQ1075—95¢)

☐ **ZENYA by E. C. Tubb.** Dumarest commands her army as the price of a bit of Earth fable.   (#UQ1126—95¢)

☐ **ELOISE by E. C. Tubb.** The twelfth of the Dumarest novels brings that rugged traveler closer to his goal.
(#UY1162—$1.25)

☐ **EYE OF THE ZODIAC by E. C. Tubb.** At last Dumarest finds a world that knows the Terrestrial zodiac!
(#UY1194—$1.25)

☐ **JACK OF SWORDS by E. C. Tubb.** Dumarest's fourteenth adventure—a life for a single cue!   (#UY1239—$1.25)

☐ **SPECTRUM OF A FORGOTTEN SUN by E. C. Tubb.** The fifteenth novel of the Dumarest saga—and he's getting closer to Sol!   (#UY1265—$1.25)

DAW BOOKS are represented by the publishers of Signet and Mentor Books, THE NEW AMERICAN LIBRARY, INC.

THE NEW AMERICAN LIBRARY, INC.,
P.O. Box 999, Bergenfield, New Jersey 07621

Please send me the DAW BOOKS I have checked above. I am enclosing $_____(check or money order—no currency or C.O.D.'s). Please include the list price plus 35¢ a copy to cover mailing costs.

Name_____

Address_____

City_____State_____Zip Code_____
Please allow at least 4 weeks for delivery

Presenting JOHN NORMAN in DAW editions . . .

☐ **SLAVE GIRL OF GOR.** The eleventh novel of Earth's orbital counterpart makes an Earth girl a puppet of vast conflicting forces. The 1977 Gor novel. (#UJ1285—$1.95)

☐ **TRIBESMEN OF GOR.** The tenth novel of Tarl Cabot takes him face to face with the Others' most dangerous plot—in the vast Tahari desert with its warring tribes.
(#UE1296—$1.75)

☐ **HUNTERS OF GOR.** The saga of Tarl Cabot on Earth's orbital counterpart reaches a climax as Tarl seeks his lost Talena among the outlaws and panther women of the wilderness. (#UE1294—$1.75)

☐ **MARAUDERS OF GOR.** The ninth novel of Tarl Cabot's adventures takes him to the northland of transplanted Vikings and into direct confrontation with the enemies of two worlds. (#UE1295—$1.75)

☐ **TIME SLAVE.** The creator of Gor brings back the days of the caveman in a vivid lusty new novel of time travel and human destiny. (#UW1204—$1.50)

☐ **IMAGINATIVE SEX.** A study of the sexuality of male and female which leads to a new revelation of sensual liberation. (#UJ1146—$1.95)

DAW BOOKS are represented by the publishers of Signet and Mentor Books, THE NEW AMERICAN LIBRARY, INC.

THE NEW AMERICAN LIBRARY, INC.,
P.O. Box 999, Bergenfield, New Jersey 07621

Please send me the DAW BOOKS I have checked above. I am enclosing
$_____(check or money order—no currency or C.O.D.'s).
Please include the list price plus 35¢ a copy to cover mailing costs.

Name_____

Address_____

City_____State_____Zip Code_____
Please allow at least 4 weeks for delivery